HALFBACK!

Sports Books by C. Paul Jackson

For younger boys:

BIG PLAY IN THE SMALL LEAGUE
CHRIS PLAYS SMALL FRY FOOTBALL
LITTLE LEAGUE TOURNAMENT
LITTLE MAJOR LEAGUER
PEE WEE COOK OF THE MIDGET LEAGUE
STEPLADDER STEVE PLAYS BASKETBALL
TIM, THE FOOTBALL NUT
TOM MOSELY—MIDGET LEAGUER
TOMMY, SOAP BOX DERBY CHAMPION
TWO BOYS AND A SOAP BOX DERBY

For older boys:

BASEBALL'S SHRINE
BUD BAKER, COLLEGE PITCHER
BUD BAKER, HIGH SCHOOL PITCHER
BUD BAKER, RACING SWIMMER
BUD PLAYS JUNIOR HIGH BASKETBALL
BUD PLAYS JUNIOR HIGH FOOTBALL
BUD PLAYS SENIOR HIGH BASKETBALL
BULLPEN BARGAIN
FULLBACK IN THE LARGE FRY LEAGUE
HALL OF FAME FLANKERBACK
JUNIOR HIGH FREESTYLE SWIMMER
PASS RECEIVER
PENNANT STRETCH DRIVE
MINOR LEAGUE SHORTSTOP
PRO FOOTBALL ROOKIE
PRO HOCKEY COMEBACK
ROOKIE CATCHER WITH THE ATLANTA BRAVES
ROSE BOWL PRO
SECOND TIME AROUND ROOKIE
SUPER MODIFIED DRIVER
WORLD SERIES ROOKIE

HALFBACK!

by

C. PAUL JACKSON

HASTINGS HOUSE, PUBLISHERS

NEW YORK

Published simultaneously in Canada by
Saunders, of Toronto, Ltd., Don Mills, Ontario

ISBN: 8038-2649-4
Library of Congress Catalog Card Number: 70-170631
Printed in the United States of America

For Butch, Gerrie, Julie and Betsy

Table of Contents

CHAPTER ONE

The Whole Picture

RANDY FLETCHER stood in the hall outside Brad Barton's room. He was short, blond and round-faced; he always tried to seem business-like in anything that involved the MIDLAND U DAILY COLLEGIAN, as befitted a sophomore sports editor of the DAILY. He clutched the folded sport section of a city newspaper in one hand while he knocked briskly with the other. He disregarded a door-muffled shout from within and knocked again.

The door opened. Brad Barton said, "I yelled that it wasn't locked and to c'mon in."

Brad was in slacks and a T-shirt that stretched

taut across his deep chest. His black hair was tousled. "Guess I was half asleep, listening to a dumb TV show," he said. "How come you knocked at all?"

Randy Fletcher looked up at Brad, down at the newspaper and back to the taller youth. "This isn't exactly a social call," he said. Randy unfolded the sports section. A headline stretched across the front page: BRAD BARTON NOT TO RETURN TO MIDLAND NEXT YEAR.

"The editor-in-chief is going to want to know about this crazy thing," Randy said. "Me being sports editor, I have to talk with you about it."

A stubborn wariness came into Brad Barton's dark eyes. He shrugged shoulders that seemed almost as wide as they did when encased in shoulder pads and football jersey. "It's no crazy thing," he said. "So what's to talk about?"

"You aren't denying it?"

"It's true. The newspaper guy asked me to give him something about how I saw prospects for Midland football next year. I just told him I had no thoughts on that because I wouldn't be at Midland next year. I can't see that I've let out any big thing. It's no big secret; I'm just not coming back."

"Is this tied in with the statement Coach gave to the wire services?" Randy asked shrewdly.

"In a way, but only a small way."

"How small? Anything you say is off the record, if you want it that way."

"No reservations." Again Brad shrugged. "Quote from his statement: 'Our spring practice has not been impressive.' Then the usual guff about next year's tough schedule, every team gunning for Midland, loss of key men. Then quote again: 'As for help from the freshman team, the outlook is not encouraging. Brad Barton has been given an overrated buildup. He stood out in frosh games, true. But it is more likely that he will be cut down to size when he faces varsity competition.' Unquote."

Randy Fletcher said, "There has to be more than that, or you're putting yourself in the position of an if-I-can't-be-quarterback-I'll-take-my-ball-and-go-home sandlot kid!"

"Okay, maybe I am." Brad's features tightened. "How many guys would feel like cheering when they read stuff like that? So, I wrote it off as mostly excessive zeal on the part of sports writers; maybe the kind of stuff any coach would put out to protect himself. Then he began needling me every chance he had. He'd refer to 'false alarms' and 'scholarships that could better be used by real tough football men.' Well—nuts!"

"Yeah." Randy Fletcher inclined his head. A frown wrinkled his round face. "It's hard to understand why Coach would downgrade you after the Alumni Game. For sure you looked good then—and most of the guys who come back and play for the alumni have had pro experience. They really put out because as they say, they don't like to be taken by kids.

I've heard varsity men claim that the annual Alumni Game to end spring practice is tougher than most games during the regular season."

"Maybe he got on me because I showed him up at the Alumni Game," Brad said. "I knew that he couldn't take away my scholarship, but do you have any idea how uncomfortable things can be made for a guy on scholarship if the top brass wants to move him out? Ask your dad sometime—the Graduate Manager of Athletics has to know. Anyway, I am not returning to Midland next fall, and neither Mr. R. C. Fletcher nor anybody else can change that.

"If and when I do come back, it will be on my own. The outfit my dad works for has a fleet of merchant ships sailing all over the world. I have a job on a ship starting the Monday after my final exam. I figure to save enough dough to pay my own way, when and if I decide to come back to college. Dad agrees because he thinks a nineteen-year-old will mature a lot being on his own. Mom is so teed-off at the stuff put out on national wire services by dear Coachie that she wants me to go to some other 'institution of higher learning' in her words. The only thing that concerns you and the sports writers is that I probably will be somewhere on the other side of the world when football men report next year."

Randy said, "Off the record: the fact that Coach yanked you from the Alumni Game and kept you on the bench more than two quarters contributed some to your decision, I take it."

Brad considered, and then answered: "You could say that. He chewed me good about tipping whether I was going to pass or run. I didn't believe it then and I don't believe it now. When he put me back in the game in the fourth quarter, I suppose I was keyed higher than a kite. Anyway, never before did I run sixty-two yards from scrimmage on an option play for a touchdown, then pitch a thirty-yard pass to a receiver who completed a fifty-one-yard scoring play. After the game I laughed at Coachie and told him those alumni guys must have been playing blind for years not to see that I tipped plays whenever we were going to score! I guess that was probably going a little far in rubbing things in. But it all adds up to Brad Barton having a bellyful of Coachie!"

Brad Barton had newspaper clippings—even whole sport sections—sent him during the year he was serving as a deck seaman. He knew when he came back that he had said no word to anybody about Midland's football coach after the talk with Randy Fletcher. But as the season progressed and Midland U experienced a dismal season, Brad also knew that sports writers, television sportcasters and alumni had really worked "Coachie" over. Alumni groups had adopted resolutions condemning him for "driving away the best prospect Midland U had in years." Soon the alumni were demanding the coach's scalp.

Brad picked up a batch of papers in Singapore and the sports sheet of one flatly predicted that: R. C.

Fletcher, Graduate Manager of Athletics at Midland U, is negotiating a settlement of the remainder of the present football coaching regime. Our bet is that within days, the coach will "resign."

Brad did not learn until after he had forwarded an application to the Midland U registrar, and been accepted for re-enrollment, that R. C. Fletcher had personally selected Mike Ryan as Midland's new headcoach. Later he wondered whether he would have gone back to Midland if he had known that Ryan would be in position to say whether Brad Barton played or not.

Sportswriters and photographers crowded the athletic offices; flash bulbs popped almost continuously. Randy Fletcher thought, *the "little" press conference Dad arranged for introducing Coach Ryan and reintroducing Brad sure took.* Someone asked Brad Barton how he felt about the upcoming season and if he was in condition after a year away from training.

"It would be hard for a deck seaman not to keep hardened and physically tough." Brad grinned. "I have a faint recollection that the way I answered a previous question about an upcoming season did nothing but bring grief to a lot of people. But I have to say that I'm rarin' to go. Don't write this as a prediction— but I honestly feel as though this will be a tough year for Midland opponents."

Then he looked at head coach Mike Ryan and

was abruptly recalling the day that Ryan tried to sell him on going to the local junior college.

"Contrary to what you think, Barton, I am not talking entirely from a selfish viewpoint. You would get more competitive game experience playing two years of junior college ball than you would playing on a freshman squad a year and probably putting in more bench time than playing time your sophomore year. Two seasons with us would count only one year eligibility-wise. So what have you got to lose?"

"What would I have to gain? A fellow gets used to the system his freshman year. I can make a big-time squad. I've had offers guaranteeing that I'll PLAY *as soon as I'm eligible. Why waste two years?"*

"You're a good prospect," Ryan admitted. *"But there is general agreement among top coaches that the time to play a sophomore as a starter is when he's a junior. They need coaching and game-experience to smooth rough spots and smarten up. We just might be able to do things for you, Barton. You aren't a finished back, you know."*

Superlatives thrown around his name in sport-sheets and on television sports shows were as vivid then as now in Brad's mind. . . . Capable right now of playing in a college backfield. . . . A complete player. Adequate passer, hard-running and mobile ball carrier, exceptional kicker . . . Where did Ryan get that good-prospect-not-a-finished-back crack? Who did this coach of a peanut outfit hardly a step above high school coaching think he was? Okay, maybe he shouldn't have laughed; maybe he shouldn't have been quite so cockily confident.

"What do I lack to be a finished back?" he asked. "What do you think you just might be able to do for me?"

"Does that mean you'd consider staying here at home a couple of years?"

"I have no ambition to be big in a little set-up!"

"Sometimes turns out to be little in a big setup. If that's your decision, let's leave it to Midland U coaches to catalogue your shortcomings."

There in the athletic office, Brad experienced the same irritation toward Ryan as he had before. He said, "I'm hoping I can help make things tough for the other teams—that is, if Coach Ryan hasn't catalogued so many faults for me already that I don't make his team."

A flicker across the back of Ryan's eyes showed that he knew exactly what Brad meant. No one else did. Newspapermen looked at Brad, at Ryan and then at each other. Someone asked, "How about you, Coach?"

"If a coach goes around making over-optimistic predictions, he's going to be in a bad way if he needs a crying towel later," Ryan said. "Barton was great in high school when I was familiar with his play and his frosh year at Midland is a matter of record. I anticipate no need for catloguing any of our players' faults."

R. C. Fletcher frowned, then boomed, "Of course, Barton and Coach Ryan will get along! We're going to have a great season. Now, you boys would like to get a few action shots of Barton—I had the equipment manager lay out one of our new home uniforms, and Brad will go through his paces, I'm sure."

After the newspapermen left, Randy Fletcher laid a hand on Brad's arm outside in the hall, detaining him. "Just a sec," Randy said. "I'd like a special word, just anything we can run in the DAILY that won't be in every other paper that subscribes to wire services or—"

"I hope I'm wrong." The voice of R. C. Fletcher came to them through the open transom above the office door. "Did I sense a certain edginess between you and Barton?"

"If there was any edginess it came from Barton," Ryan said.

A small silence. R. C. Fletcher's tone sounded grim when he said, "I'm going to be frank, Ryan. I personally recruited Brad Barton and we have a stadium to fill in order to pay off bonds and maintain our athletic programs. Those are two facts to keep in mind, along with another thing—colorful stars attract football fans.

"Brad Barton is a rugged individualist; it's part of his color. He has ability to go along with that color. Maybe he should be treated a little differently than the run-of-the-million youngster. Barton will draw crowds to see him play, Ryan. I hope you understand."

"In plain English, Barton is to be pampered at any cost?" Ryan asked.

This time the silence was longer and when Fletcher spoke his tone was definitely stiff. "Your statement is unnecessarily crude," he said, "but substantially correct. Extension of your contract beyond this year may well hinge on your—ah—tractability in the matter of Brad Barton."

Mike Ryan spoke gently, almost as though thinking out loud. "I suppose I should feel properly put in my place," he said. "But the contract I signed as head coach has no clause that says I must get a green light from you for what I do."

"Now, see here, Ryan! I am not attempting to put you in a green-light-from-me position. That attitude will get neither of us anywhere!"

"Let me finish." Ryan's voice did not rise. "I'm not looking for a battle with anyone. I realize your power and influence and I'll be as frank as you. It's been a long pull to get to be head man of a big-time football squad. I don't intend to throw away any opportunity by high-handed treatment of Barton—or anybody else—merely for the satisfaction of showing who *is* head man.

"I know Brad Barton, probably better than you. I intend to develop a winning football team and Barton figures largely in my plans for that team. But it will be a *team*, not a vehicle for exploiting any one man."

Randy Fletcher glanced up at Brad. "Yeah," he said and nodded. "There's a look at the whole picture, I'd say."

CHAPTER TWO

A Small Inner Voice

TEN DAYS AFTER Brad Barton reported for the Midland U squad, Western Aggies would come to Midland Stadium to open the schedule. It was a non-conference game, but important as an intersectional test. Coach Ryan and his staff bore down, doled out white shirts to a second string aggregation the sixth day of practice and called a scrimmage. After designating a varsity eleven offensive unit, Ryan spoke briefly to the squad.

"Nobody should think permanent starting selections have been made nor that any position is sewed up by anyone. We are beginning with the nucleus of letter men and reserves up from last year. I want to emphasize that any man who shows he can produce for Midland better than another man in any position will be moved ahead. Blue team take the ball on the forty. We'll work on offensive timing."

Brad Barton grinned and said in a low tone to Whitey Martin, "The time-honored bromide that every position is wide open."

Whitey did not grin. "Sounds like he means it, I think."

The scrimmage was as lacking in smooth performance as most early scrimmages are. Ryan and his assistants patiently pointed out errors, had plays run over and over until the timing began to take on a semblance of rhythm. After a half hour no suggestion had been made to Brad Barton. Then Ryan instructed Brad to mix up the plays, use the triple option as he would in a game.

Brad faked a pass and carried the ball himself off-tackle. He sliced through for eight yards behind a crisp block thrown by Al Haney, burly fullback.

"Nice," Ryan said. "Blocking like that wins games." He turned to Brad and added, "Your timing was perfect. You hit the hole at exactly the right instant."

"Thanks," Brad said in a cocky tone. "Maybe I'll get by in spite of my faults."

The instant the words were out, Brad wondered why he had said them. Ryan just seemed to rub him the wrong way, but there was no excuse for a guy to spout off. Oh, nuts! The coach could have mentioned something about the way Brad Barton ripped and pivoted out of a tackler's arms.

Ryan ordered a pass. Brad faked a pitchout, faked running himself, scrambled until Bill Jones maneuvered clear behind the free safety in the defensive backfield. Brad's pass to the wideout receiver was right on target. Jones ran to the three-yard line before he was shoved out of bounds.

The head coach turned the teams around, and said to Brad, "We're a touchdown ahead, three minutes to the end of the half. It's fourth and one from the forty-eight. You call it."

The varsity hepped into punt formation from the huddle, Brad in the kicking spot. He got off a high spiral that hit on the twelve and rolled out of bounds at the six. Ryan called, "Varsity ball again. Same situation."

Brad was surprised when the coach came near and said in a low tone, "An alert defense might have blocked that kick. You tip when you're going to pass or run and you give away when it's a punt."

Brad just stared. Here it was. That old line about cataloguing faults. "I get by pretty good," Brad said.

Ryan's expression was quizzical. He said, "Mix 'em up." He went behind the second-team line.

The varsity trotted from the huddle into the wishbone-T set that Ryan had installed. Just before Turk Lauter handed Brad the ball, Coach Ryan called out clearly, "A pass. Watch it, Whites!"

White-shirted players tacked onto eligible receivers; the front four linemen rushed Brad hard. He twisted and dodged and sheer clever footwork nearly brought him clear, but a linebacker got to him—a six-yard loss.

"Luck!" Brad snorted in the huddle. "Guesswork. Option sweep to Al, from 42B. Let's see some downfield blocking. Hep!"

Again just before the ball was snapped Mike Ryan called warning to the defense. "He's running it!" The second team ganged Al Haney after the big, tough fullback made only two yards.

On the next play, Ryan called, "Fake pitchout. Watch Carnes and Haney for short pass!"

Chuck Carnes caught the swing pass out in the flat but the cornerback and safety on that side corralled him at the scrimmage line for no gain.

"It's still luck!" Brad fumed in the huddle. "I'm going to pass from punt formation. Get open!" He can't guess 'em all!"

"Be nice to have a guesser like that on our side," somebody muttered.

They hepped into punt formation. Brad Barton seethed inside. Let Ryan call this one! He was going to look plenty bad.

Ryan waited for the second "Hut!" from Brad. Then the coach shouted, "Pass! Pass! Watch the pitch, Whites!"

The White ends and linemen charged, rushed Brad and an end trapped him when he attempted to scramble. An eight-yard loss. Coach Ryan blew his whistle.

"Scouts use powerful glasses and they miss very little," the coach said. "They're a cinch to spot a man tightening the fingers of his throwing hand when he's going to pass—no matter how slight the motion. You can't allow your eyes to shift even a teeny when you're going to run and the small movement of a kicker's foot when he's going to punt is sure to be noted, unless he makes it every time whether he kicks or not.

"That's all. Everybody once around the field before you hit the showers."

Whitey Martin finished the jog around the field beside Brad Barton. Whitey did not waste words. "You had that coming," he said. "Ryan was decent, tried to let you down the easy way, but you figured you'd show him up. He had you over a barrel and every right to chew you plenty. I never noticed the things he called you on, but you must have been doing them for him to have been tipped. He called exactly what you were going to do. In my book, Ryan leaned over backward to give you a square shake."

Brad sat staring at the study table, frowning, not actually seeing the table. He had been painfully reconstructing mental pictures of the Aggie game. Finally he took a newspaper clipping from the table drawer. Mom had insisted since high school days on pasting any piece with mention of Brad Barton in her scrapbook—books by now. This one he'd clipped from the Sunday paper, but he wondered whether he would

send it to his mother. He read the newspaper piece
again. The part that made it a doubtful addition for a
scrapbook was several paragraphs below the heading.

BARTON SPARKS 14–9 MIDLAND WIN
OVER WESTERN AGGIES

. . . . Brad Barton was replaced at quarterback
early in the third period, right after a weaving, twenty-
six-yard scoring dash on a beautifully executed quarterback draw play. A successful point-after-touchdown put
Midland on top, 7–6. Two Aggie field goals accounted
for all first-half scoring and fans were wondering about
highly touted Midland U.

Midland's defense blunted another Aggie drive
midway of the fourth quarter, but a third Aggie field
goal gave the westerners a 9–7 bulge. Brad Barton returned to the Midland lineup for the kickoff following
the Aggie three-pointer. . . .

Brad scowled at the clipping. Weren't sports writers supposed to delve into things? Not a word about
Mike Ryan jerking him out of the game because he
called an audible to replace the play the coach sent in.
Didn't the fact that he went through for a touchdown
prove that the Aggie defense had been set for a sweep?

*Yeah, but that was the third or fourth time you ignored
plays he sent in. The guy IS coach, you know!* An inner voice
suddenly sounded off in Brad's consciousness.

So what? The quarterback out there in the action
sees things they can't from the sideline, or the press
box.

*Even pro coaches send plays in to veteran pro signal
callers!*

It's hard to beat a touchdown result when it comes to quarterback calls.

Take that third-down sweep that Ryan sent in. Okay, so it was the fourth quarter and a field goal would have put us ahead—if things worked out. Say it would have gotten the ball somewhere near the midpoint between the hash marks and set up a better angle for a fourth-down field goal attempt, if it didn't make first down. Part of a quarterback's job is to read defense. Right?

The middle linebacker was definitely leaning toward the strong side, and the safety edged over that way. They smelled a sweep coming. What was wrong with changing the play at the line of scrimmage? The quarterback-keep off-tackle slant ran cross-grain to the flow they expected and broke up the secondary. The touchdown we scored for sure was better than position for a field goal try!

Yeah, and they could have smeared you and it would have been a tough angle for a field goal try against that cross-wind.

Brad crumpled the clipping and hurled it toward the wastebasket. How could a coach rationally bench a fellow for running the winning touchdown?

Rationally? Could you be rationalizing some now?

Oh, shut up! Brad did not say the words aloud, but he was thoroughly disgusted with the inner voice. He did not exactly care for the uneasiness it brought on. Things were bad enough when a fellow had to battle a coach determined to chop him down.

CHAPTER THREE

Star on the Bench

I can save this ballgame. Send me in and let me play my way and I'll win it for you, Ryan!

Brad Barton did not say the words aloud as he hunched his shoulders beneath his pads and wriggled restlessly on the Midland U bench. But the set of his chin, the straight line of his mouth and the stubbornness in his dark eyes showed that he was unrepentant of actions that had put him where he was.

"Sins?" Brad Barton snorted when a newspaper feature writer asked him before the game if he was not sorry 'for the sins that forced Coach Mike Ryan to bench you.' "Is it a sin to play the way you have always played? Ryan should know that a guy out there in the action knows what he is doing a lot better than a coach on the sideline. I won the Aggie game last week, sinning like that!"

Out on the field, Steve Barr, second-string quarterback was still uncertain at being shoved into the signal-calling job in an important conference game. He half crouched behind the broad posterior of center Turk Lauter and barked, "Twenty! Thirty-two! Twelve! Fifty-four!"

Barr's eyes shifted from side to side, trying to read the Gulf U defense as he shouted the numbers. Brad Barton leaned forward. Only one person who had not been in the Midland huddle could know what the upcoming play was, but from the string of four even numbers the team and Midland players on the sideline knew that Barr saw nothing in the defensive alignment to warrant calling an audible—an oral sign which would automatically change the play to a different offensive setup. Midland was going with the play given in the huddle.

He'd better not call an automatic, even if he sees the defense stacked, Brad Barton thought. *Mr. Iron-glove Ryan sends in a play, you run* THAT *play, or else!*

"Hut! Hut! Hut!"

Barr took Lauter's handback, ran three steps backward as though to pass, then pitched out to a halfback. A swelling groan came from Midland supporters in the big stadium as a linebacker and the cornerback met the ballcarrier when he tried to turn the corner. Gulf U's defense had diagnosed the sweep perfectly.

"We want Barton! We want Barton! We want Barton!"

The cry from the Midland student section of the stadium increased in volume as fans in other sections joined. The chant was not new. It had become a roar a week ago during the Aggie game. Brad Barton glanced along the bench toward the thick-set man in street clothing at the other end. Mike Ryan, in his first year as head coach of Midland U football, sat staring out at the players on the field.

Nervous? How could he be otherwise?

Ryan *had* to be getting the message from the stands. But no one would have guessed that he consciously heard the rhythmic yelling. He lifted a battered, faded hat that might have once been green and momentarily exposed his thinning brown hair.

"Martin!" Coach Ryan suddenly called the name of the blonde-haired boy who sat beyond Brad Barton. "Get ready. If we don't make the first down this play, go in and kick that ball a mile. Stay in at strong safety."

"Me?" Whitey Martin stared wide-eyed at the heavy-shouldered man. "Gosh, Coach, I can't punt anywhere near as good as—"

"Get ready." Ryan gave Whitey Martin a level look. "Or can't you take orders either?"

Martin's eyes turned toward Brad Barton, then

back to the coach. "Yes, sir," he gulped. "I'll be ready."

For just an instant Mike Ryan's gaze met Brad Barton's and there seemed to be a question in the coach's gray eyes. Brad's pulse quickened. Ryan must be recalling that it was Brad Barton who straightened out Whitey Martin on a couple of things he was doing wrong in trying to punt. Why, Ryan had admitted that Brad did a better job by demonstrating kicking technique than a coach could do by merely pointing out mistakes. He must know that Whitey was still uncertain; that he could not match Brad Barton by at least ten yards even when he got off his best effort. Ryan was making a final bluff calling Whitey. Mr. Iron-glove was going to *have* to come to it!

Then Ryan's gaze returned to the field with no further sign of awareness that his star player sat on the bench. The referee checked the position of the down indicator between the end markers of the linesman's ten-yard chain. "Third and seven," the official called.

Whitey Martin jogged behind the bench, swung his kicking leg every few steps. He passed behind Brad and spoke in low tone. "Tell him," Whitey urged. "Tell him you're sorry and that you'll be good. We gotta have you in there, Brad, or our season's shot before we really get under way!"

Brad Barton blinked rapidly. It made him mad to realize that tears like those he had experienced in kid-league football games were almost in his eyes. His chin quivered. For an instant he was more vulnerable than he had ever been as a kid.

Then the quiver stilled and his eyes hardened. He ran long fingers through his black hair. They were fingers that could pitch accurate passes or curl around a football tucked against his chest. For that matter they could reach up and destroy enemy passes, too, a heck of a lot surer than Whitey Martin's. But they could do Midland U no good from the bench.

Coach Ryan had sent in instructions to run a draw-play instead of the third-down pass that might be expected. But the middle linebacker read the draw all the way. He stopped the ball carrier after a scant yard gain. Whitey Martin ran out and took the deep position for a punt.

Now in his third season as Midland U center, Turk Lauter had never made a bad snapback to his kicker. But this time the Gulf U man opposite Turk got away with a foul. He drove forward before the ball moved; his arm hit Lauter's hand an instant before the snap was made. The leather oval sailed way wide and thirty inches over Whitey Martin's head.

Whitey leaped desperately, tipped the ball, lunged and managed to grasp the oval. But a towering Gulf lineman bore down on him; Whitey had no chance to get off any kind of kick. He swerved away from the lineman but a charging linebacker hit him solidly and hard from the other side. The ball popped from his hands straight into the arms of the big lineman. The Gulf U giant lumbered right on twenty-seven yards into the end zone.

The successful point after touchdown changed figures on the scoreboard to read Gulf U, 17; Midland U, 7.

The Gulf kickoff was brought back to the Midland thirty. Brad Barton eyed the big electric scoreboard at the open end of the stadium horseshoe. One minute and thirty-four seconds of playing time to the half. Plenty of time to engineer a scoring drive. Going into halftime intermission behind 17–14, a team would be much more still-in-the-game than going off the field ten points down. Brad threw a glance toward Mike Ryan.

Ryan's hat was pulled low on his forehead; his broad, rugged face set in bleak lines. Steve Barr also glanced questioningly toward the coach. Mike Ryan made absolutely no sign. Barr trotted out with the offensive unit.

Brad Barton scowled as he looked out on the field. A short flip from Barr to Chuck Carnes coming out of the backfield was complete over the line for a first down. Sure, Gulf was in a prevent-defense now, willing to give the short-yardage gain to eat up time on the clock.

Less than a minute to the end of the half.

There was a try to shake Carnes loose on a sweep, with less than five yards gain. Steve Barr ran the option-play from a Wishbone-T setup. A hole opened momentarily off tackle just as Barr chose to pitch to Carnes rather than keep the ball himself. The underhand toss was poorly timed; Carnes was forced to slow and reach back for the ball. And the Gulf rover-back hurled his bulk across the gap and stopped the ball carrier cold.

"Arr-r-a-a-a-a-u-u-u-u-g-h!"

The formless roaring growl from the stands rolled across the field. Fans could be remembering the identical setup in the Aggie game when Brad Barton kept the ball, darted through the line, broke past secondary defenders and sped forty-three yards into the end zone.

Barr came right back with the option-play and the defense was confused enough so that when Barr faked a pitchout, faked keeping the ball and then ran diagonally back to his right, two wide receivers were well down-field. But the Gulf safety men refused to be fooled. A long pass designed for a scoring bomb was knocked incomplete, nearly intercepted. Fourth down and five. Another short pass completed—time ran out before the receiver could get out of bounds.

Brad trotted glumly toward Midland's team quarters. He had just turned into the ramp that led to the dressing-room tunnel when somebody heaved a rolled newspaper over the barrier, along with a derisive jeer:

"A Midland U year, the man says! Year of the Big Collapse, that is,—phooey!"

Brad scooped up the newspaper without breaking stride. Then he thought: *reflex action from a year of continually policing ship or having some officer character chew on you.* He unrolled the paper, saw it was a copy of that day's MIDLAND U DAILY COLLEGIAN. A headline stretched across the front page. BARTON BENCHED: BARR AT QUARTERBACK. A subhead below asked: *Ryan Depending Too Heavily On Defense For Midland U Year?* By Randy Fletcher.

Brad folded the paper, ready to shove it in the trash can outside the dressing room door. He did not need to reread the piece below the byline. Randy Fletcher made things clear enough so that one reading was plenty. Brad Barton had only himself to blame for being benched—even though Randy Fletcher questioned Mike Ryan's expressed confidence that Midland's defensive unit would hold Gulf U in check and Barr would lead the offensive to a win.

Well, take a setup with the editor of the college paper being the son of R. C. Fletcher, Graduate Manager of Athletics. You could expect that the Establishment—the coaches and staff of the athletic department—would never come out short in the DAILY COLLEGIAN.

CHAPTER FOUR

Maybe a Long Season

BRAD BARTON shunned the benches provided in the dressing room. He had had all the bench sitting he wanted for a while. He leaned his elbows on a locker-room window sill, facing players as they sat or stretched out on gym mats on the floor.

Trainers and coaches moved about, tending bruises and abrasions, pointing out mistakes made in the first half, handing out verbal pats-on-the-back to some players.

An unaccustomed emptiness held Brad inside. Nobody paid any attention to him. He tried hard to not stare at Mike Ryan and Steve Barr holding an earnest conference. But there was just no way he could keep from looking their way again and again.

That pigheaded Ryan! Still hidebound to old ideas from his junior college coaching days; still refusing to accept what sports writers said about Brad Barton's "fabulous three-year high school grid career," or the unanimous appraisal of college recruiters that his football potential was in the "can't miss" category.

It ought to be Brad Barton out there talking over second-half strategy with Mike Ryan ! Finally the coach turned from Barr and stood staring at the floor.

"All right, everybody." The words from an assistant coach shattered the comparative quiet of the dressing room. Brad saw that the assistant had been watching Mike Ryan for a signal. "We're about ready to go out for the second half. Coach Ryan has a few words to say—listen!"

Brad Barton wondered if he was being fair to Ryan as he thought, *the guy sure knows the value of timing. He's waiting for absolute quiet.*

Ryan stood in the center of the room and let his gaze roam for a couple of seconds, then began speaking in a low tone that barely carried over the rumbling crowd noises outside.

"I have never been very good at dressing-room oratory," he said. "I played my college football under a coach who did not believe a team can be brought to peak performance simply by dishing out a die-for-dear-old-Alma-Mater fight-speech. Problems cannot

be solved through attempts at psyching up a team between halves."

Brad was sure that Mike Ryan eyed him a notice-
able space of time as he paused and swept his gaze over
the dressing room.

"You are a squad that has high potential," the
coach went on. "It may be that your potential has
been blunted by lack of coaching efficiency—that remains to be seen. I tell you now that if you go out there
and play the football that you are capable of playing,
you can pull this game out."

Head coach Mike Ryan again paused. His eyes
turned briefly toward the window beyond the lockers.

"If everybody doesn't start putting it all together,"
the coach continued, "if we don't start playing up to
our potential—then it may be a season that seems
longer than our schedule indicates!"

Brad Barton sat on the bench throughout the
third quarter. He squirmed and wriggled while Midland's offense sputtered and misfired and failed to dent
Gulf U's defense. Gulf's attack never let up their re-
lentless pressure. The over-worked Midland defense
unit started to crack. A fatal fact became increasingly
clear—no defense can function at top level when there
is not sufficient time between on-the-field stints for rea-
sonable rest. Midland's defense unit began to tire
badly toward the end of the third quarter when the
offense unit failed to make a first down.

Twelve minutes of the final quarter were gone when a Gulf man came out of the backfield and grabbed a pass in the area Whitey Martin was supposed to cover. Whitey stumbled and fell, trying desperately to reach the receiver, and the Gulf man failed to score only because he inadvertently stepped out of bounds.

Suddenly Brad Barton was down in front of Coach Mike Ryan, without really realizing he had jumped from the bench.

"Send me in there for Whitey!" Brad scowled. "He's had to punt so many times and make so many open-field tackles that he's worn out!"

Mike Ryan looked out on the field, hesitated briefly then nodded at Barton. "Report in for Martin," he said.

Brad drew on his quarterback experience as he took the strong safety position. Mostly opposing quarterbacks reason that if a substitute is better for whatever position he comes to fill in, he would have been the regular at the job. Besides, the man coming in is usually cold and more or less uptight as any sub is. So, hit him with a play before he has opportunity to get settled down and loose.

"Okay," Brad muttered to himself. "Try it on me and I'll show you I *am* better!"

He watched the play develop. The Gulf tight end —the receiver who is the strong safety's normal assignment to cover—slanted to the opposite side. But also the split end was running a cross-over pattern that would bring him into the strong safety's area.

Brad waited, apparently indecisive, then at the exact right instant dashed in front of the split end. The pass was just a little under-thrown and Brad had to dive to make the interception at the Midland twelve-yard line. He had no chance to get up and run before the Gulf intended receiver was on him.

Midland's ball. The offense unit would take over. Brad looked hopefully toward the sideline, but Steve Barr, Chuck Carnes, Al Haney and Bill Jones were coming out for the offensive backfield.

Two Midland plays and time ran out. The conditional statement Mike Ryan made in the dressing room between halves ran through Brad's mind. . . . it may be a season that seems longer than our schedule indicates. . . .

No "may be" about it. Unless Ryan came to his senses it *would be a long season.*

CHAPTER FIVE

Two Visits

THE KNOCK on his door came a second time after Brad said loudly, "It's not locked. C'mon in." Randy Fletcher stood in the hall when Brad opened the door.

He looked up at Brad, nodded and said, "Yeah. Kind of a rerun from an old show."

"Okay," Brad said shortly. "You always knock twice when it's not-exactly-a-social-call. Cut loose."

"Yeah." Randy nodded again. "Skipping any build-up, you're all wrong, Brad. Deep down you know it, I think. Mike Ryan is not going to knuckle to you. He is a knowledgeable football man; he is fully aware that benching you takes away at least fifty per-

cent of Midland's offense. But you remember the way
he stood up to Dad after that phony press conference
Graduate Manager of Athletics R. C. Fletcher arranged to exploit Brad Barton.

"Brad, I've done some research on Mike Ryan
since then. I tell you right flat out—Mike Ryan is not
a man to carry a prima donna on his team!"

"Randy, you're editor of the DAILY COLLE-
GIAN; you're a newspaperman. Corn-merchanting
just is not a newspaperman's style. You know as well as
I do that coaches keep their jobs by turning out winning teams."

Randy Fletcher sucked in a breath, regarded
Brad and shook his head. "You sound just like Dad,"
he said. "I can't buy the thesis that college football is
just to fill stadiums, regardless of what it does to the
guys who play it. *Play* it? If you and Dad are right,
then college football as an amateur sport is a big fat
lie! I still believe there is more to it than win, win, win!
If that makes me a corn-merchant, then that's what I
am!"

"Cut it out!" Brad protested. "Not the old charac-
ter-building bit. Please! Look at the colleges scram-
bling to recruit football players every year!"

"Does the fact that some colleges surrender and
become football factories make it right?"

"About that prima-donna crack." Brad did not
answer Randy's question. "It fits Ryan better than
me!"

Randy Fletcher was silent a space of time. Finally he shook his head. "You're wrong as wrong," he said. "Ryan wants to play you; the team needs you. But the thing is you've set yourself up as the Great-I-am-Glamour-Boy—or something. You got one coach fired, so now you expect Ryan to knuckle to one player's desire for self-aggrandizement! Ryan will never do that, even if it costs him the job my dad handpicked him for."

"Hey, wait up a sec!" Brad defended himself. "I never tried to get anybody fired. I'm not trying to run Ryan. He's the coach. It's just that—"

"Just that you're too big to be whittled down by a man who has coached only at the little junior college in your home town." Randy Fletcher finished for Brad. "You've always been the kingpin. If you were not directly responsible for Midland's coach being fired last year, it was because of you that Dad maneuvered the man into resigning and taking a cash settlement for the remainder of his contract.

"Okay, so you are admittedly the key to Midland hopes this year. Sit back and take an objective look at your place in the picture. It isn't pretty, Brad!"

An hour later Mike Ryan could not mask his surprise when he answered his door buzzer. He eyed Randy Fletcher and Whitey Martin questioningly.

"I phoned earlier," Randy said, "But you weren't in. We would appreciate a few minutes, sir."

A quirky little half-grin lifted the corners of

Ryan's mouth. "Anybody who calls me 'sir' after yesterday's near-disaster," he said, "is welcome. You must
have phoned while I was at the office going over scouting reports from Tunsani U's game. Come in, a coach
always has time for the press."

Whitey Martin blurted, "I'm not connected with
the DAILY, Coach. It's just that—that—well, I guess
I'm out of line!"

"You know Brad Barton's background," Randy
said. "That's why we're here. Just in friendly interest,
we want to know about Brad."

"Just in friendly interest?"

Whitey Martin shifted weight from one foot to the
other. "I'm for Brad," he said. "We roomed together
our freshman year. I like him. But I wonder whether
being for Brad is really being for the team."

"Seems a little odd that a roommate should be
asking about Barton."

Randy Fletcher said, "Don't let's spar, Coach.
What we mean is that business of keeping Brad out of
the offensive unit today, among other things."

"Brad's not a swell-head," Whitey said. "He's
cocky, but it's never been the kind of cockiness that
riles you. More like he's just doggone confident. Sometimes Brad is kind of meek. Another thing that bugs
me is that I just don't understand the way he's been
since he came back after missing a year."

"We figured maybe we would get a better slant on
Brad if we knew his background thoroughly," Randy
contributed.

"You fellows sound a great deal like some psychology professor testing a theory. Put it down that playing Barr at quarterback was a move I've been considering. Barr is a senior and deserves his chance. He came up to my expectations, too." Mike Ryan frowned, then went on slowly. "You must understand that there is no deep, dark secret in Barton's background, nothing for any soft-pedal stuff. But I'm trusting you both to not make public what I say."

Randy and Whitey nodded.

"Brad Barton was endowed by nature with exceptional physical ability and coordination. Also, he owns a drive that pushes him constantly. Part of that drive comes from his mother—her background. I'll explain."

Again the quirky half-grin twitched Ryan's face. He chuckled.

"As a kid in high school," he went on, "I had a crush on his mother—before she was a mother. A typical adolescent puppy-love crush on a beautiful girl, along with half the boys in our high school.

"Edith Smith, now Mrs. Barton, was an actress all the way. She was good enough to get to Hollywood, but she never quite made the grade to stardom. It was not because she lacked assurance, the self-confidence that most artistic people have, believe me."

Ryan stopped for a moment and then went on more as though explaining something to himself, "Probably she projected herself into Brad with a determination that he would get to the top she did not quite reach."

Then he went on. "She came back to her home town and taught Dramatic Art in our high school. When she married she broke the hearts of a lot of boys. When she bore a son, she raised him in the tradition of her own self-confidence, that's for sure. The boy was applauded for every accomplishment. You could say that he could not avoid being cocky. Under the circumstances, it would have been miraculous if Barton had not acquired an exaggerated ego. He just has never learned that there has to be something more than self in the whole picture."

The quirky little grin flickered around Ryan's mouth.

"Brad's full name is Vincent Bradley Barton. His mother even picked that name according to the all-conquering thesis. 'Vincent' comes from the Latin and means 'a conqueror. Invincible.' The story in our town was that she wanted to give him Arnold for a middle name, from the Teutonic meaning 'eagle power', but Brad's father insisted he be named Bradley because it is an old name in his family. Barton was called Vincent when he started to school, but for some reason he preferred being called Brad."

Ryan stopped and seemed to be lost in thought. Finally he said, "Barton will be All American calibre when he learns that no matter how good you are, you're dependent on others to a degree by the very nature of things. He has to learn that a man sometimes must submerge himself for the good of the whole effort."

Randy Fletcher asked, "Are we right in believing that you intend to make Brad realize that? You won't let pressure from Dad change you?"

"Mr. Fletcher and I want the same thing, maybe for different reasons." Mike Ryan's tone was sober. "He wants a winning team that will draw crowds. I am more concerned with coaching each boy to his best effort, to turn out the best team I am capable of turning out with the available material."

"But it will be a *team*." Randy Fletcher said. He met the sharp look from Midland's head coach. "Yes, sir, you're right." Randy admitted. "That's a direct quote. Brad and I overheard you telling my father that the day of the press conference."

"Then Barton and you also heard my game-plan for our season?"

"No, sir. Photographers yelled for Brad and we went on down to the dressing room."

"Just as well Barton didn't hear." Ryan divided a steady look between Randy Fletcher and Whitey Martin. "This is definitely off the record for your DAILY, Fletcher, and if anything shows that you leaked to the squad, Martin, I'll have your heart!"

"Yes, sir."

"Of necessity," Ryan said, "we have had to go along with the system favored under the coaching staff last year. Incidentally, I talked with the man I replaced before I agreed to come to Midland. He realizes that he allowed resentment toward R. C. Fletcher to warp his treatment of Barton. He was very bitter about

Mr. Fletcher taking over everything down to recruit-
ing.

"In any case, I intend to develop what I call a
flexible offense, eventually. I want Midland to run
from three or four sets, such as Power I, Wishbone T,
single or double wing on occasion. We want to run an
offense shaped along the lines of Michigan State's multiple attack. But it will take time—and I have to say
frankly that a good bit of the success or failure of my
season game-plan hinges on Brad Barton."

Randy Fletcher said, "I swing a little influence on
the DAILY, and I have no hesitation on using it. You
can count on me to help in the levelling-off process on
Brad Barton."

"You can count on me, too, Coach," Whitey Martin said.

CHAPTER SIX

In the Orange Bowl

BRAD BARTON, wearing Number 17 in blue numerals on his traveling jersey, stood between the five- and ten-yard lines and looked up the field. He could not truthfully say he was entirely happy over the shift Mike Ryan had made, leaving Steve Barr at quarterback and putting him at halfback. But it was better than being on the bench. For sure a lot better, if Ryan was going to continue using his quarterback as an on-field robot who fitted into a rigid pattern of dependency-on-the-bench for play calling.

Brad looked around at his teammates. Without conscious volition he yelled, "Nothing to worry about, gang!"

47

Chuck Carnes, the other halfback, was moving about in a tight circle; big Al Haney, usually as stolid as the bull his great bulk resembled, shifted weight from one foot to the other. Players ahead of the potential receivers of the kickoff all were moving around restlessly.

What the heck? It was no different from a kickoff to start any old game!

But being set to receive the initial kickoff of the Tunsani U versus Midland U game *was* different. It was being played in the Orange Bowl. Brad looked up at the lettering on top of the West end-zone stands. LWOB EGNARO IMAIM from down here, MIAMI ORANGE BOWL when read approaching the huge stadium outside.

The Orange Bowl. Home of the annual Orange Bowl Classic between top college teams New Year's night; scene of home games of the Miami Dolphins, a power in the American Conference of the National Football League; frequently hosting the pro Super Bowl game. Cleats of many gridiron immortals had bitten into the artificial turf that covered this playing surface.

Brad Barton chuckled, almost laughed aloud. *You're doing a hero-worship job on yourself to stave off the jitters.* He never had suffered pre-game jitters, but things combined to make this a little different. *Snap out of it. We could be back down here New Year's Day night. Ryan may be coming alive. Win this one and the Old Dominion thing and go on through the conference and—whoa, Barton! You're getting a chance to start, but who can know what Ryan will pull next?*

Just boot that leather apple my way! I'll show Ryan and everybody that Brad Barton is still Brad Barton—halfback or quarterback—only more so!

The referee raised a hand toward Midland. Captain Turk Lauter glanced at the men ahead of the restraining line with him, then at teammates behind. Turk lifted a hand and inclined his head. The Tunsani captain signified they were ready and the referee dropped his arm while he shrilled his whistle to signal that the opening kickoff was under way.

The kick was end-over-end and high, coming down a little to Brad's right. He yelled, "Mine!" He moved smoothly in line with the descending oval, held back just the right amount of time and was in full stride when he grabbed the ball as an outfielder fields a baseball when he is going to make a throw to a base.

He started upfield behind the blocking wedge, saw that a Tunsani flanker was cutting in too quickly. Brad tucked the ball under his arm, left the blocking pattern and barreled for the clear outside path.

Suddenly it was not clear. The Tunsani end reacted fast, shifted back. Chuck Carnes threw a block at him, too late. The Tunsani man knocked Brad out of bounds at the Midland thirty-two. Chuck Carnes limped off the field as Whitey Martin ran out to replace him.

"We were knocking their guys over pretty good,"

Turk Lauter said to Brad. "Might be an idea to try following your interference."

"I wouldn't have got this far through that jam down the middle!"

Barr called a trap play between guard and tackle. Tunsani linebackers smashed Al Haney to the ground after a bare two-yard gain. A play from Ryan was brought in by way of an offensive guard, one of the shuttle Midland's coach used to send in plays. Tunsani did not expect the play and there could have been a substantial gain, but the hole was a fraction of a second late in opening. A linebacker dumped Brad almost as quickly as he was through the line. Third and seven.

Ryan sent in the same play. In the huddle, Steve Barr chirped, "Let's go! Make it good, Barton!"

Al Haney threw a block on the Tunsani linebacker and the guard and tackle were partially boxed, but the smoothness that the play required just was not there. Brad was hit by a safety barreling into the center lane and the ball was still four yards short of first down. Whitey Martin came in to punt.

The kick was very close to being blocked. The ball brushed the fingertips of a leaping Tunsani man but still carried to their thirty-five where it rolled out of bounds.

Tunsani made only six yards in two running plays and their third-down pass was smelled out by the Midland defensive secondary and knocked down incomplete.

Tunsani punted out of bounds on the Midland nineteen.

"We roll!" Steve Barr barked in the huddle. "42 Red. Make it sharp once."

The power smash off-tackle did not unwind right. The timing was off, the hole opened too late. Brad Barton improved nothing by yelping at the Midland tackle and guard when they came into the huddle. "If you guys can't open a hole at least get out of the way so a guy won't stumble over you!"

Pete Smith, a big, ungainly but effective tackle, looked at Ray Parson. The stubby guard shook his head. Brad thought Parson muttered, "Cool it, like Whitey said."

Barr called a halfback pass. His pitchout to Brad was perfect. Brad made the play as deceptive as he could but Tunsani was not fooled. It was almost as though they knew what was coming. Linemen came through in a terrific pass rush. Brad looked frantically for a receiver open; there was none. He heaved the ball deliberately high and out of bounds in the general direction of Mick Rooney.

Al Haney powered to within two yards of first down but that deep in their own territory, Coach Ryan refused to gamble for the necessary yardage and Whitey Martin went back to punt. Once more the Tunsani line rushed hard and hurried his kick. Whitey barely got it away.

Brad Barton fumed. Doggone it, he was much

quicker than Whitey at getting off a kick, and Ryan had to know that.

Then it was as though the game followed a preconceived script. Tunsani could not make their first down, and punted. Midland's offense sputtered and Whitey Martin punted. The first few minutes seemed to set the pattern for the whole first half.

For brief stretches Midland looked like the powerful offensive machine that experts had predicted. But their attack was rough and inconsistent. Something always happened to bog down their drive.

Midway of the second period Brad Barton chased down a surprise Tunsani quick-kick and ran the ball back to the Tunsani twenty-nine. Then for three plays the offense clicked. Al Haney bulled up the middle for five. The burly fullback came right back and slashed inside tackle to mere inches short of a first down. Ryan sent in a play that was a dandy call.

The defense set quite obviously was intended to combat an expected smash into the line to pick up the short yardage first down; the option pass that Steve Barr flipped was right on target to Whitey Martin and caught the defense off-balance. Martin was only a step from the goal line; a defensive back came racing across too late. All Whitey Martin needed to do was grab the ball and step into the end zone, but the leather oval slithered off his hands—straight into the grasp of the Tunsani back diving desperately to cover. He clutched the ball an instant before he tumbled to the turf and then slid over the sideline of the end zone.

Touchback.

Tunsani's ball on the twenty-yard line. Just under three minutes of playing time to the end of the second quarter showed on the scoreboard clock.

Tunsani's offense reacted to the interception as though it was a shot of adrenalin. Line smashes, off-tackle slants mixed with short passes, marched Tunsani to three consecutive first downs. A sideline pass connected and the receiver carried to the Midland eighteen. The clock moved into the final minute of play before the end of the half. Midland's defensive unit dug in. They held Tunsani to four yards in three plays.

With eight seconds showing on the clock, Tunsani lined up for a field-goal try. The Midland defense prepared to rush all-out to block, or at least hurry the kick so it might go wide. Then as the holder grabbed the snap from center, the play unfolded as a fake field-goal try. The man who normally would have placed the ball in position for the kicker leaped erect, sidestepped charging linemen and whipped a beautiful pass to a teammate standing in the corner of the end zone with no defender closer than six yards.

Touchdown!

The point-after kick hit an upright of the goal post and bounced off to the side. No point. Tunsani took no chances of a long runback, and sent a squib kick skipping along through the front men. Mick Rooney, tight end, fielded the ball and was swarmed under after a six-yard return, and the half ended.

"I had a sure touchdown," Whitey Martin wailed as the teams trotted toward the tunnel to the dressing rooms. "So I took my eyes off the ball and blew it! Instead of six points on the board for us, I opened the gate for Tunsani!"

"If we don't get with it next half," somebody said, "we're playing OUR bowl game right here a couple of months before bowl-game time!"

CHAPTER SEVEN

On a Big White Charger!

BRAD BARTON stood in front of the bench for the second half kickoff, seething inside. He had watched Mike Ryan during intermission. Ryan spoke quietly, pointed out mistakes, remarked that things like dropped scoring passes were breaks of the game and breaks could be turned around by a determined team.

He said not a word to Brad Barton. When the three-minute warning came, Midland's head coach nodded and said, "We'll be kicking. No changes in the defensive unit. When we get the ball, the same offense unit that started, except that Martin will be at running back with Haney, and Jones will be in for Carnes."

Brad was stunned. He still felt numb as he watched the defense hold Tunsani and force a punt. Migosh, Ryan *couldn't* do this to him again! He looked toward the coach, hoping that Ryan would change his mind. Mike Ryan gave no indication of awareness that Brad Barton was even in the Orange Bowl.

What could a fellow do? Ryan had been the whole cheese in the jerkwater junior college, so he had to be the whole cheese now. Well, it could turn out that his cheese smelled!

Ryan sent in 49 Red for the first play, the bread-and-butter off-tackle slant. It was not far from the old crossbuck, really, with a halfback taking the handoff and cutting across according to the direction of the play; Red to the left, Blue to the right. Whitey Martin fumbled the handoff like an overanxious high school boy. Al Haney beat a Tunsani man to the loose ball but it cost Midland a three-yard loss.

"We want Barton! We want Barton! We want Barton!"

The contingent of Midland students was small in the huge Orange Bowl but they were vociferous beyond their numbers. Their chant sounded full and demanding. Mike Ryan looked down the bench. Brad Barton reached for the zipper tab of his warmup jacket. Ryan called, "Carnes!"

Brad stared incredulously. Ryan must be completely out of his skull. Carnes had hobbled all week with a hip bruise and he had re-injured himself when he threw a block on the kickoff. It was crazy to risk him again.

"Out there for Martin," Ryan said. "Tell Barr to run 42 Blue."

The coach met Whitey at the sideline. "Take it easy," Ryan said. "You're nervous. Sit down beside me and watch a play or two."

Either Carnes told Barr the wrong play or somebody misinterpreted something. Bill Jones half-fumbled the hand-off and lost a yard frantically recovering the ball. Brad Barton groaned in sympathy with Jones, but his sympathy was drowned by a savage feeling that it served Ryan right. The crazy fool!

A pass was incomplete. Martin went back in for Carnes, who limped more than ever as he came off the field. Time ground away and still Brad Barton sat on the bench. The rhythmic chant from the Midland contingent in the huge stadium sounded louder and louder; Brad wondered if fans other than Midland supporters were joining. It could be they have heard about Brad Barton down here. Maybe they—come off of it, Barton! Could also be you're getting as egocentric as Ryan! The chant from the stands continued.

"We want Barton! We want Barton! We want Barton!"

The electric scoreboard clock registered fifty-nine seconds of play left in the third quarter when real disaster struck Midland.

Tunsani owned the ball on their forty, third down

and six. Brad Barton yelled a warning as Tunsani came from the huddle. "Watch a pass out there!"

His diagnosis of Tunsani plans proved all too right.

A Tunsani back sneaked down the sideline as their split end and tight end ran crossover patterns. *Not the ends. They're decoys! Get that back slanting out!*

Brad did not know whether he yelled out the warning, but he knew that the Tunsani men down the middle were bait to suck the Midland secondary and they fell for it all the way.

The Tunsani passer stopped abruptly, whipped a long spiralling pass that his receiver took over his shoulder on the Midland twenty. He cantered on unhindered into the colorfully lettered Midland end zone. But the back judge signaled other officials. No hands were raised above the head of any man in striped black-and-white shirt. A yellow flag stood out against the green of the artificial turf at the eighteen-yard line.

A Tunsani man had clipped there. The fifteen-yard penalty placed the ball back on the thirty-three. Brad Barton let out a breath. Breaks had a way of evening, but—he glared toward Ryan. The score was still 6–0 against Midland as the fourth quarter began.

"We want Barton! We want Barton! We want Barton!"

The chant from the stands became angrily demanding as the final period began. Ryan HAD to come to a realization of the fans' desire. But Mike Ryan kept his attention on the action out on the field as though he were deaf. Twelve minutes to play. Ten. Nine.

Brad Barton was suddenly in front of head coach Mike Ryan. Barton's expression was more worried than defiant. "What's the idea," Brad demanded. "Are you trying to give it to Tunsani!"

"You're blocking my view. Sit down."

Barton plunked angrily to the bench beside the coach. "Don't you want to win?" Brad demanded. "Do you want Midland to take a licking before a national television audience?"

"I've never been conditioned to take a licking anywhere." Ryan eyed Brad briefly. "Is a Midland win your primary concern, Barton?"

"What are you talking about! Of course winning is my first concern. You're costing us another game because of a whole-cheese complex!"

"The on-television angle doesn't enter your head, I suppose."

"Who are you trying to snow? You're costing your team a game because of I'm-the-boss thinking! You resent it because I don't bow and salaam to you and—"

"You've never been more wrong," Ryan cut in. "Do you really believe any coach would sit and watch his team flounder around and keep a player on the bench because of personal feelings—if he believed that man could change anything?"

"We want Barton! We want Barton! We want Barton! . . ."

The insistent yelling from the stands beat around their ears. Brad Barton said challengingly, "Hear that?"

"I hear." Ryan's tone was grim. "I saw your play the first half. You didn't follow your interference; you raved and ranted at blockers because you were looking bad. You simply refuse to learn from mistakes."

"What mistakes? I got the ball in scoring territory running back that quick-kick!"

"And you ruined the halfback pass by your same old tipping habit! Mistakes!" Ryan spat. "I'm the one who doesn't learn by mistakes! It was a mistake to think that you might have matured after a year of being on your own! The biggest mistake I have ever made is trying to treat you as a young man with some maturity, while you're still basking in the aura of best-high-school-prospect-in-the-state!"

Ryan, looking Brad Barton squarely in the eyes, went on.

"Your concern right now is not primarily whether Midland wins or loses. Your head is full of that 'We want Barton!' In your view, you have to get out there somehow to show your public that Brad Barton is the fair-haired lad on a big white charger!"

Ryan bit off his words and his eyes stabbed deep. He said harshly, "Well, let's see you do it! Give the boys a chance to help you and they'll smear you with glamour. All right, you're a destiny's boy hotshot. You can play defense and offense and obnoxious! Get out there!"

Brad Barton was entirely aware of the roar from Midland supporters in the Orange Bowl. He felt the old lift that applause had always given him. But he felt something else—a smarting from Ryan's tirade, and a determination to show him once and for all.

Tunsani owned the football, third and two on their own forty-six. Logic dictated a line play to pick up the first down. But Brad remembered a similar situation when Midland threw a pass. He saw the Tunsani quarterback eying him surreptitiously. Brad edged a couple of steps closer to the line and saw that the quarterback noted his move. Brad owned a sudden conviction that the new-guy-is-not-as-good-as-the-man-he-replaced-or-he-would-have-been-in-here syndrome was in the Tunsani quarterback's mind.

The play started as an orthodox smash and Brad took two more steps in as though he was convinced it was a line play. From the corner of his vision he saw a Tunsani back drifting out into the flat zone and he was not surprised when the quarterback stopped and pivoted and tossed a lateral to a halfback.

The halfback-option-pass was by no means an invention of Mike Ryan. Brad pumped his long legs toward the Tunsani man out in the flat as the lateral floated across to the Tunsani halfback.

Brad timed the thing perfectly. He leaped in front

of the Tunsani back, glued his fingers around the ball and his legs were pistoning as he hit the artificial turf.

A pass out in the flat zone always carries the danger of backfiring on an interception and well-coached teams attempt to provide insurance. Tunsani had two men racing to cover. Brad sized up the defense. It was going to be close. One man he could out-maneuver, but two was a different setup.

He cut for the center to gain needed space then abruptly executed a cut-over step and jammed a stiff arm into the first tackler. He pivoted free, but it took a precious second of time. The other tackler pinned him to the sideline, a cinch to knock him out of bounds very soon.

"In! Cut in!" The gasping words came from behind Brad Barton. "Drag a little and give me a shot at him!"

Whitey Martin. Brad danced a step outward, cut back sharply as the tackler closed in. Whitey Martin's stocky bulk hurtled through the air and wiped the Tunsani man completely out of the play.

Brad Barton rode the crescendo of yells from the Midland supporters down the sideline. He was going all the way. Try this on your junior college fiddle, Mister Mike Ryan! One play and I'm putting your football team back in the game!

But he did not score a touchdown.

Evading the tacklers had slowed him just enough

so that the Tunsani passer had time to angle across for a desperate tackle try at the eight. He did not hit Barton squarely and the Midland ace's driving power broke the tackle, but in staggering to regain balance, Brad Barton stepped on the sideline chalkmark at the five.

First down; five yards to a touchdown. Midland was full of pepper in the huddle.

"Time we rolled! . . . Everybody's hitting! . . . It's yours, Al. Bust in there!"

Al Haney blasted into the center of the line. The Tunsani forward wall yielded a little, only a yard. Oddly no play came in from the Midland bench. Steve Barr glanced at Brad and said, "They'll figure Barton for this one. We'll fake it. Al spin-bucks that thing in!"

Al Haney masked the spinner well and there was a slit of daylight through guard, but a linebacker sensed the fake and flung his bulk to block the hole. The ball was still two yards short of the double chalkmark when Haney got up. Barr said in the huddle, "42 Red. Give him a hole, you guys. Barton's earned this one."

The off-tackle smash had not been working all day. The timing had not been right; it was not right this time. The hole opened too soon and was closing as Barton spun into it. He churned his cleats and the sheer power of his drive slammed him through a tackler. Another Tunsani man hit him, and another. But when the referee dug to the bottom of the pile of scrimmage, the ball was smeared with the white of the goal line.

Touchdown!

The kick for point after touchdown was blocked. Scoreboard figures blinked to Tunsani, 6; Midland, 6. Six minutes left to play was registered on the clock.

Tunsani received; they ran for one first down as the clock light flicked into the four-minute circuit. They came from their huddles slowly, apparently willing to settle for a tie. They were finally forced to punt and they prudently kicked out of bounds to kill any chance of a runback. It was Midland's ball on their own thirty-two with less than two minutes to go.

Sixty-eight yards is a lot of mileage to cover in two minutes, when a team's offense is sputtering as Midland's was this night.

It sputtered again now. Haney off-tackle for three; Barr on a sneak for two; Barton a scant three on 42 Red. Tunsani expected a pass when Haney bulled his way up the middle for the first down.

But now the clock was in the last minute.

Tunsani went into their prevent defense, willing to give up short yardage to prevent a scoring bomb or long gainer. Barr passed complete to his tight end but Mick Rooney was downed after eight yards.

A draw play netted first down on the Tunsani forty-three. Whitey Martin had never kicked a field goal beyond thirty-five yards. A guard came in with a pass play from Ryan.

"They'll know it's a pass," Brad Barton said in the huddle. "It's got to be a pass. But let's fox 'em."

"How could we fox them? They've seen everything we have. Besides, Coach sent this one in."

"Show them something we haven't got. Whitey, you drag out to the side and sneak down the sideline. Al takes it, fakes a plunge, then drifts wide to give Whitey time. Don't cut it too fine, but hold off as long as you can then shoot the ball back to me. I'm going to heave it all the way, Whitey. Get under it!"

Steve Barr stared at the flashing-eyed star. He said shakily, "But Coach sent in the—"

The made-up play unwound like a coach's dream. Haney barging up there confused Tunsani momentarily. Their linebackers and secondary reacted to meet the threat. When the fullback swerved and drove wide, the defense followed. Nobody noticed Whitey Martin speeding down the sideline. Haney was all but tackled before he pivoted and shovel-passed back to Barton. "Pass! Pass!" Tunsani defensive backs yelled suddenly. But Whitey Martin was twenty yards away from any defensive man.

Brad Barton did not throw the ball sixty yards, but it was a pass high and straight. Whitey Martin turned at about the twelve, ran back a few paces and gathered it in. The nearest forlorn Tunsani man was fifteen yards away as Whitey circled into the end zone, holding the ball high.

The try-for-point was good. Midland, 13; Tunsani, 6.

Brad Barton raced for the dressing room tunnel, slowed as he passed Mike Ryan and grinned triumphantly.

"On a big white charger," he yelled. "All smeared with glamour!"

CHAPTER EIGHT

Whitey Lays Things on the Line

FACED EACH DAY with columns of blank space to fill, sports writers try to give their readers what they want. It is the nature of sports fans—football branch—to want their major reading to be about the scorers of touchdowns, the makers of spectacular pass catches, the kickers of field goals. Brad Barton made the headlines of Sunday newspaper sports sheets after the Tunsani game. Not a single pressbox observer failed to comment that Midland U's offense came alive in the Orange Bowl only after Brad Barton came into the backfield in the final quarter.

The MIDLAND U DAILY COLLEGIAN did

not publish a Sunday paper, but Brad's name was conspicuously absent from the Monday DAILY's account of the Tunsani game.

It happened that Whitey Martin and Brad Barton picked up copies of the DAILY COLLEGIAN at the Union news stand about the same time. Brad stared at the headline.

'M' COMES FROM BEHIND TO TAKE TUNSANI. MARTIN'S SENSATIONAL CATCH OF LAST MINUTE PASS CLIMAXES WIN.

He flicked a quick glance at Whitey, read further down the game story.

> Midland's play was generally ragged, especially on offense, but gave evidence in spots that Coach Ryan is developing a team that will hold its own in conference competition . . . the smoothness of execution that a team reaches in mid-season cannot be expected at this stage. . . .
>
> Midland supporters can be proud of the manner in which the team fought back . . . a team victory . . . no one man deserving of credit for the Orange Bowl effort before a national television audience . . . Whitey Martin's key block on the lengthy run preceding Midland's first touchdown and his catch of the long, last-hope pass in the waning seconds merit some mention. . . .

"What gives, Whitey," Brad said half-joking, half-serious. "Did you make a contribution to the DAILY's budget, or something?"

"There for sure wasn't anything sensational about that catch." Whitey did not look comfortable. "Seems as though they were trying to make the squad feel good. There are a lot of references to the team."

He did not bear down heavily on the final word, but Barton caught the slight emphasis. He said, "Something kind of lurks behind that profound observation, huh?"

Whitey Martin hesitated, then said, "Meet you here after class. Randy's section of Journalism IV is in the same building where my eight o'clock meets. I'll bring him along."

"I can't wait to see the budding journalist!"

Apparently not many students had seen the DAILY, or if they did, had missed its subtle propaganda. As Brad Barton crossed the campus walk toward the Science Building for his eight o'clock psychology class, dozens of greetings came his way. "Great stuff in Miami. . . . Man, did you ever pick us up! . . . Looks like you're making an early bid for All American! . . . Sure lighted up the television tube. . . . Way to go, Big Man! . . ." Brad basked in the plaudits. He was all smiles, waves of a hand, laughing answers to quips.

The psychology professor always held Brad's interest. Frequently he tied some campus activity into his lecture, or some happening involving Midland U. But he made no reference to any such thing this day. Most of his lecture had to do with the psychology of self-delusion and rationalization.

"Every personality holds in his own self the mechanism of rationalization. . . . can be a form of self-hypnosis. A practiced rationalizer can establish scores of acceptable reasons for doing a thing he wants to do, but shouldn't do. . . . . devices for not doing that which he should do but does not want to do. . . .

After the class ended, Brad Barton was again the recipient of verbal pats on the ego out in the corridor. He did not brush off any of his admirers but he did break away as quickly as he decently could. He was anxious to get to the Union.

Whitey Martin met him on the steps outside the Union building. "Randy's holding down the back booth," Whitey said and hesitated a moment before continuing. "Look, Brad, I want you to know beforehand that I'm on Randy's team. Include me in on whatever gripe you make!"

Brad shrugged, but after they carried their cokes to the rear booth where Randy Fletcher sat, he wasted no words. "Who," he asked the DAILY editor, "is the character on your staff who's sold out to your honored Mike Ryan?"

"Sold out? What do you mean?"

"It's very simple. You're editor of the campus scandal sheet, so you're responsible for what goes in it. I mean that Big Cheese Ryan finagled somebody into fronting for him in type."

"It may be simple, but I still don't get what you're driving at."

"Did you read the masterpiece your sheet put out on the Tunsani game?"

Randy looked at Brad, looked at Whitey and said softly, "I read it—before it was set in type. Mike Ryan had absolutely nothing to do with it. I wrote that piece myself."

"*You* wrote it!" Brad's expression was incredulous. "What's the large idea?"

"Okay." Randy Fletcher drew in a breath and then expelled it. Briefly he told of the visit he and Whitey Martin paid Coach Ryan. He recounted Ryan's request that what he told them was not to be made public and assured Brad that they would keep things confidential.

"But I believe all the way that you are wrong as wrong to battle Ryan," Randy finished. "The DAILY believes that the *team* deserved credit for taking Tunsani. You could say that we're trying to save you from yourself, Barton."

Brad did not miss Randy's use of his last name. He stared at the DAILY COLLEGIAN editor and then suddenly threw back his head and laughed.

"They must dish out screwy stuff in that journalism class," he said. "Would it be out of line to ask what you're going to save me from—oh, yeah, you said myself! Well, I say you're ladling out corn. Overripe corn!"

Randy Fletcher's chin lifted. His clear blue eyes steadily held Brad's black ones.

"I think you know we can mow you down some," he said. "You need to—"

"Don't tell me, let me guess!" Brad interrupted. "I need to learn that Brad Barton is only a small-town flash. I've got to become a shrinking violet. Even when I'm good I have to give credit to everybody but me." He snorted. "It's a crime for a guy to have confidence in himself!"

"It isn't like that," Randy said quietly. "Self-confidence is wonderful. But you'd better know that we're starting a campaign to tone down the Brad Barton Glamour-boy myth. You—"

"Hi, Whitey! And Brad! Great stuff down in the Orange Bowl!" A trio of entering students shut off whatever the DAILY editor was going to say. "Did you see that crummy piece in today's—" A companion yanked the speaker's arm and said in a loud whisper, "That's Fletcher with them. He's editor of the DAILY!"

"Oh! Well—I don't care! That thing stinks. Not a word about how Brad went in there and—"

Again the belligerent student was shut off, his companions jerked him away and the three moved on.

"Quite an effective campaign you're running," Brad said as he eyed Randy Fletcher. "Have fun!"

Barton kept up the pretense that he thought Randy Fletcher was "full of corn," but underneath he was more than a little bothered. Midweek came an editorial in the DAILY COLLEGIAN titled "Fairness." No names were mentioned and it was cleverly written with just enough campus jargon to appeal to the student mind.

A coach is hired to coach. He digs when and if any
given player can serve the interests of the team best. . . .
It's stupid to yell we-want-so-and-so. So, cool it. If the
coach didn't dig his boys better than we in the stands
can, he would not *be* coach. . . .

Brad waxed bitter to Whitey Martin about the
editorial, and ended with: "I hope Fletcher is having
fun!"

"You told him to." Whitey answered.

"Can you imagine Fletcher letting Ryan talk him
into putting such a crock of corn in his paper?"

"Randy told you that Ryan had nothing to do
with what he put in the paper before. I don't figure he
had this time, either."

"Nuts! Ryan's a smooth operator, that's all. He
sold you guys a bill of goods!"

Whitey eyed him silently for a moment, then said,
"Ryan is building a team. We've looked better this
week in practice than last. He's been playing you at
halfback in the starting unit; he's had you working out
at punting. Why can't you get it out of your nut that
he's after your scalp? He's had Steve working the option halfback pass more and more, hasn't he?"

"It's not through choice, you can bet. Ryan found
out in Miami that he doesn't have an offense without
me!"

Whitey gave him a long look, then shook his head.
"Chew that remark over to yourself a couple of hundred times," Whitey said. "Maybe if you can get

through the bloated ego you're showing, you'll begin to see what Randy is trying to make you understand.

"Don't gripe to me. I'm for anything that will make us a winner—and laying things on the line, I have to say one of the main things is to whittle you down to size!"

CHAPTER NINE

Campus Thoughts

BRAD BARTON kicked at a pile of leaves as he walked alone across the campus. What the dickens was the matter with him?

He had played three years of kid-league football, ten games a season. There had been twelve games in two seasons of junior high play, thirty games in three high school years, six frosh and two varsity games at Midland U, and never had he felt real unease or tension preceding a game. But here was Brad Barton, the day before the squad would fly out to Old Dominion to meet the perennial gridiron power, as restless and jumpy as a guy trying to stay in a whirlpool bath when the water was too hot.

He deliberately swung off the sidewalk to kick at another pile of leaves.

It was warm enough for windows of dormitories to be open. He could hear bull sessions in noisy progress and for a moment wished he had stayed in his dorm and got into one himself. But that wouldn't have been any good. He would not have been able to take the coolness that had come between him and Whitey Martin.

He passed East Dorm and heard his name through an open window. He stopped and listened.

". . . than Brad Barton. Let me make it clear that I have nothing personally against Barton. It's just not healthy when one man figures the rest of the team should play primarily to give him a chance to grab the glamour train. I go along with the DAILY COLLEGIAN; it *is* stupid to yell we want Barton. We do Coach Ryan an injustice intimating that his judgment is second place to ours. . . ."

Brad recognized the voice of a senior, very active in campus affairs and with a knack of swinging student opinion. He was tempted to go in and tell the guy off, maybe punch him in the mouth. But he did not go in. Why dramatize the jerk? That line of baloney wouldn't fool anybody. He jammed his hands deep in his pockets and stalked on down the street.

Coach Ryan, Coach Ryan, Coach Ryan! First Fletcher, then Whitey and now a windy campus politician ballyhooing for him. Where did Mike Ryan get such standing all of a sudden? He wouldn't have gotten the Midland coaching job if R. C. Fletcher hadn't figured him to bring out the best in Brad Barton.

Hah!

Where would Ryan rate right now if Brad Barton had not won the Aggie game and pulled him off the hook at the Orange Bowl? It would serve the so-and-so right if something happened that Ryan couldn't shove him in there to save the bacon.

Brad Barton was abruptly playing with the idea of faking an ankle injury or something so that Ryan would not be able to play him against Old Dominion.

Hey, hold up! You couldn't do a thing like that. Why would you think of such a schnooky deal?

Barton was so intent on self-examination that he failed to notice an approaching car as he started to cross the street. He was almost in front of it and would surely have been hit but for his hair-trigger reflexes.

He heard the horn, caught the blur of movement in his peripheral range and leaped backward all in the same second's fraction. But he was off balance when he landed. His left foot slid off the curb; his whole weight was thrown on the awkwardly twisted ankle. He felt a wrench of pain stab upward through his leg.

The car stopped and the driver was frantic when he saw whom he had nearly hit. He insisted on driving Barton to his dormitory. Brad pooh-poohed the idea, assured the man he was in no way to blame, and brushed off his almost tearful apologies.

"I'm okay," Brad said. "Just twisted my ankle a little. Nothing to worry about."

He was not really concerned about the ankle at the moment. He was busy thinking. What was it the psych prof said the other morning? . . . a good rationalizer can think up perfectly acceptable reasons for doing a thing he wants to do. . . . devices for not doing what he does not want to do. . . .

Had he rationalized wanting to fake an injury so strongly that when he consciously rejected the idea, his subconscious took command and seized a way for doing what he wanted to do?

CHAPTER TEN

Old Dominion Decision

FAMED FOR FOOTBALL teams consistently ranked among the Top Ten year after year, Old Dominion was in "a building year," not a championship one. But they exhibited the fight that was traditionally ingrained in Old Dominion teams. They battled Midland U all the way.

Mike Ryan's team played much more smoothly than they had played against Tunsani. They dominated play from the opening kickoff. Yet in spite of the fact that they spent practically all of the first three periods in Old Dominion territory—and Old Dominion failed to penetrate deeper than the Midland thirty—

time inexorably drained away in the final quarter with the goose egg on the scoreboard for Old Dominion matched by the one for Midland U.

Brad Barton sat on the bench, his strained ankle tightly bandaged. All through the game he fought a mental battle. The ankle was strong enough to hold up while he went out there and pitched a pass or two. A part of him wanted to do just that. This bench sitting was not for him. Why not tell Ryan that he was good at least for part-time play?

Yeah, go in and pull out another one! You wanted to show Ryan where he stands without you, didn't you? The small voice inside had not recently offered observation but now it did. *How long are you going to keep that show-him gimmick?*

Shut up!

The scoreboard clock registered nearer and nearer the final gun. A Midland drive bogged inside the fifteen when a hashed-up pass was nearly intercepted, a backfield-in-motion penalty nullified a touchdown run and cost five yards, and Al Haney smashed through for a first down on the four, only to have the ball knocked loose. Old Dominion recovered the fumble.

Old Dominion nursed the ball, took as long as possible in each huddle, clearly willing to settle for the moral victory of a scoreless tie. But they were forced to kick the ball away while just under two minutes to play showed on the clock. A replacement at safety came out with the Old Dominion defensive unit.

"Barton!" Mike Ryan called sharply.

Brad's pulse leaped. He bounded down in front of the coach. He owned a sudden gloating joy! Old Big Cheese must be choking at having to admit he did not have an attack without Brad Barton.

"Can you go out there for one play?" Ryan asked.

Brad savored the gloating joy. Man, would he tell off this character after he won this one! He nodded.

"Report in for Carnes. Tell Barr you're to kick. Boot it straight at the safety and plenty high."

"Boot it!" Barton was incredulous. "On first down? Are you advertising that you'll take a tie! I can throw a pass to—"

"You punt." Ryan cut in. "Straight down the field to their safety and good and high. Barr will know that's an order."

Barton opened his mouth to further protest. Something about the set of Ryan's mouth and the look in his eyes changed his mind. He shrugged. Ryan lacked the guts to gamble when the chips were down. Okay, so he would go out and boot that ball a country mile and afterward he would tell Ryan off in front of the squad. But good!

Steve Barr nodded even before Barton finished giving him Ryan's instructions. "This could do it," Barr said. "Coach cautioned me that the right setup might come about that we'd pull a kick out of place. Everybody down under the kick. Put on the pressure! Hike!"

Brad honestly had no intention of disobeying Ryan's order as he stood in the deep slot. A punt in this spot was about as crazy strategy as you could think of, but he would wham that inflated leather oval over the safety's head. Then he saw the Old Dominion safety man running back and the Old Dominion secondary spreading and dropping deeper. As the snap shot back from Turk Lauter, Brad saw from the edge of his vision that Old Dominion ends were charging fast, as though they knew this kick formation was for real and not a fake.

Now they would be suckers for a fake kick and run.

He took a forward step as though kicking, then suddenly the ball was cradled in the crook of his arm and he jabbed his other hand at the leading end, used him as a fulcrum for a pivot around the other one and was clear. He raced into the broken field, slicing wide to draw the outside linebacker over and leave running room inside.

Whitey Martin reacted fast when he heard no thud of foot against leather. Whitey threw a shoulder block at the Old Dominion cornerback and Brad did not slow as he swivel-hipped around the two men. The Old Dominion safety angled across.

Brad Barton sized up the defensive picture. Linebackers and the cornerback on that side presented no further threat. Other defensive men in the secondary were too far away, except the safety. Brad turned on all the speed he had and bee-lined for the far corner.

With a sound pair of ankles he would have beaten the safety easily. But the weak ankle slowed him a bare fraction and he knew it was going to be close. The safety narrowed the gap at the two yard line and made his bid. Barton pivoted sharply—on the bad leg. The safety's hand slapped at his thighs, slid down. Barton was free.

But he was not home free. The Old Dominion man lunged desperately, got a grip on Barton's ankle and heaved. He could not quite hold the grip but he staggered Barton so that he stumbled and fell again as the jab of searing pain ran from his ankle upward. He half-dove, half-fell across the goal line just inside the red flag and the intersection with the sideline.

He lay there, grimacing with pain. *Now who have you shown up?* the inner voice asked. The trainer came out, probed gently at his ankle and gave him a blank look. "More than likely you have fixed it so you'll be out a week at least—and miss the conference opener!"

The training room in the corner of the varsity room was redolent with odors of wintergreen from the trainer's personally formulated liniment, rubbing alcohol, the disinfectant solution used to mop the floor, and the honest perspiration smell from two score husky athletes just in from a stiff workout. Brad Barton sat on the edge of the chromium tub, his left ankle immersed in the whirlpool bath in swirling 130 degree water. Air siphoned into the water enabled bruised or strained muscles and joints to stand the steaming liquid and the Midland trainer maintained there was nothing quite as effective in treating minor aches. He motioned for Barton to withdraw his foot and helped him to a training table.

Expertly the trainer massaged the injured ankle, probed with sensitive fingers. Barton winced once, suppressing a grimace. The trainer grunted and looked at Mike Ryan standing to one side.

"Just like I doped it Saturday," the trainer said. "It was strictly maybe whether rest and heat treatments yesterday and today would bring it along all that much. The heat lamp and the whirlpool have helped, but you can't heal a bad sprain all that quick. There's no use counting on using him this week, Mike."

Ryan nodded. His eyes were on Barton and his expression was grim. There was a limit to which a man could go, and this was it.

All his players knew that he gave Barton instructions to go in there and kick which would not have aggravated that bad ankle. But the thing that could not be overlooked was Barton disregarding instructions again. Ryan spoke slowly.

"You've put your team in a bad spot, Barton. Needlessly. That's the thing that counts most with me. If you have any shred of an alibi, now is the time to air it."

"Alibi!"

Brad Barton knew deep down that he was in the wrong, resented it and refused to blame himself. Ryan had no business giving such a fool order and he had a lot of brass now, coming around with a sour face when a guy had won a game for him.

"First time I ever heard of anybody needing an alibi for scoring a winning touchdown," he said cockily.

"You deliberately disregarded my instructions, Barton."

"And because I did, you came home with a ball game won!"

Mike Ryan did not raise his voice but nobody could have missed the steely undertone in it when he spoke again.

"You were a deckhand on a merchant marine ship, Barton. You must have learned that always there has to be someone in command. It happens in this instance that I have the responsibility with our football team. You won a game, yes—and you may have cost us the Mountain State game.

"I told you once, Barton, that football scouts miss very few tricks. Midland scouts are on a par with any others. One of our scouting reports on Old Dominion disclosed that a certain defensive back was inclined to press under tension. That man went in at safety just before I sent you into the game.

"Our coaching staff discussed the possibility of

playing this man's weakness; it was part of our game plan, if the occasion presented itself. You haven't entirely rid yourself of tipping when you're going to kick, and we knew that Old Dominion scouts would have spotted it and passed the information on to their players. That safety might well have fumbled and we would have had men down there to recover. Beyond all that, you were not in physical shape to take chances."

Ryan stopped briefly, then finished quietly, "Whether a man agrees with me or not, it is my responsibility. I expect my instructions to be obeyed."

"The master calls the shots and the puppets jump his way, huh?"

"I expect my instructions to be carried out."

"So, I'm kicked off the squad!" Barton's tone dripped sarcasm as he tossed out the careless remark. "That's the logical next step!"

"The decision on your future with us is yours. I've never dropped a man off a squad I coached. I've lost a few, but it has always been their decision whether they quit."

Barton flushed. "Which means I'm invited to kick myself off," he said. "You're suggesting that I turn in my equipment?"

Ryan could not have missed the stunned incredulity in Barton's eyes. The coach said, "I'm suggesting nothing. I'm merely stating my position." He turned abruptly and left the varsity room.

Big Al Haney glared at Brad Barton. "That," the fullback growled, "is par for the course. Ryan gave you a blamed sight better break than you had coming!"

"Check. . . . You deserved a real chewing out. . . . get wise to yourself. . . ."

Mutters of agreement came from other players. Barton looked around the varsity room. Not a man showed any sympathy.

"Corn!" he flared. "What's eating you guys? The object was to beat Old Dominion, wasn't it? So, I beat 'em! You ever hear of a fellow using his head and pulling the unexpected? That fumble stuff was strictly maybe—why didn't he tell me?"

Whitey Martin said quietly, "How about we all break it off? You can sneer at Ryan, Brad, call his stuff corn. But he is coach, and no coach has to detail his strategy to any player. The point is, you deliberately took things into your own hands—set yourself up as above Coach—and in my book it was a pretty school-kiddish performance. When are you going to grow up?"

CHAPTER ELEVEN

In the Television Booth

THERE WAS no sign of a limp in his stride as Brad Barton tramped around outside the stadium dressing room door. He wore slacks, open-collar shirt and the soft blue-patterned jacket Midland U provided football players this year to wear on trips. Doggone everything! This latest evidence of Mike Ryan's mulishness griped Brad. His ankle was as sound as ever. The trainer knew it and he had told Ryan. But Big Cheese majestically rode the captain-showing-a-deck-hand-who-was-in-command role today. He refused to allow Brad Barton to suit out and sit on the player's bench.

"The Atlantic game next week is Homecoming," Ryan said. "Your public will jam the stadium. If you

88

were suited out today, we might be tempted to use our game-saver—and we just can't risk disappointing your public by maybe aggravating your ankle so you could not play against Atlantic. Now, can we?"

It was the first time Ryan really brought out in the open the vindictiveness Brad was sure he felt. *What do you call the jackass stubbornness you've shown? Could you be just a little vindictive because he told you when you were a high school flash that—*

Shut up! Brad Barton dismissed the small inner voice which increasingly plagued him. He considered making an issue of Ryan's refusal to let him suit out and going to R. C. Fletcher and laying everything on the line. Mr. Fletcher would tell Ryan soon enough what was what. Or maybe go to the sports writers and wise them up that Ryan was keeping him needlessly out of the Mountain State game because of martinet pettiness. He was confident that he would come out ahead in any showdown with Ryan.

Confident? How have you done so far?

Shut up! Brad Barton wished more than once that he had slept through the lecture the day the professor in Psychology II discussed the subconscious and how it frequently injected views into one's thoughts.

What had he done, really? Truth to tell, Brad Barton was bewildered. Three or four more barbs had come out in the DAILY COLLEGIAN, and it was not just his imagination that a difference in campus attitude was emerging.

They were all nuts! A fellow committed the terri-

ble crime of winning three football games for his team
—did that turn him into a leper, or something? When
everything was boiled down, a big hunk of baloney re-
mained, no matter how it was sliced.

Barton was still milling around in the crowded
ramp a few minutes before game time. He suddenly
saw R. C. Fletcher. The Graduate Manager of Athletics' expression could only be labeled harassed. Brad
Barton touched his arm.

"Look, Mr. Fletcher," he said. "I think I'd better
talk with you about—"

"Barton!" Fletcher did not let him finish. "Just
the answer to my problem! I had a lad all picked out
and briefed to help the International Sports Television
people spot for us. Now I can't find him, he must have
got tied up in traffic, or something. They're about
ready to go. Scoot up to the pressbox, Barton, and take
over."

Fletcher had Barton by the arm before he finished
speaking and was pushing him through the crowd. He
practically shoved Brad toward the elevator to the
pressbox. "I won't forget this," Fletcher said. "I've got
a thousand things to see to right now." He wheeled
and was lost in the throng.

Brad pushed the up button of the elevator. It was
barely minutes before the kickoff. The IST sportscaster
looked around briefly when Brad came into the booth,
saw the monogramed M above the pocket of his jacket
and grunted. " 'Bout time you showed up." He lifted a

hand in a vague gesture toward another youth and said, "This is the Mountain State spotter. Hope you chums know everybody on your respective squads."

Down on the field below, a line of men in green jerseys and gold pants stretched across behind the forty-yard line; one of the Mountain State men stood several yards deeper. Midland players in spotless white pants and white jerseys with huge blue numerals on front and back, spread over their end of the gridiron to receive. The referee dropped his hand and Mountain State players ran forward with their kickoff specialist.

It was a wobbly kick to Whitey Martin. Green jerseys snowed him under at the twenty. Brad Barton listened in fascination to the rapid-fire voice of the IST telecaster.

". . . First down for Midland on the twenty. They hustle from the huddle into their version of the Veer-T offensive set made famous by Houston University. There's the snap. . . . It's a pitchout to Carnes, a sweep around Mountain State's right flank—no, no! A cutback. Carnes slants sharply and knifes into a gap but a linebacker has him cold—no! He doesn't get Carnes, he couldn't! That tackler was obliterated by—" the television man signalled frantically to Brad Barton while he fumbled with the sheet of press-radio-and-television-information that Midland had supplied.

"Martin," Brad said.

The telecaster went on smoothly. . . . "Martin. The block gave Carnes the necessary step and he went for. . . . Yes, it's a Midland first down on their thirty-six. That play was good for sixteen yards, fans, and very pretty to watch. I'm sure that Mike Ryan could not have asked for better execution. . . ."

There was scarcely a break in the staccato comments. The telecaster always had something to pass on to his listeners.

"Now it's the Power I set. This Ryan has installed a truly multiple offense at Midland. They run from the Veer-T, the Power I, Wishbone T and sometimes a double-or single-wing formation. . . . Al Haney takes the handoff from Barr and churns up the middle. Almost another first down, but not quite. Make it second and a short yard. Now, Carnes has the ball. He's cutting sharply, he's—no he isn't! Looks like maybe a busted play. Carnes was hit behind the line of scrimmage. Third and about two, the third-down hook that stabs every quarterback, the most crucial down in football. Can Midland keep this initial drive going? Or will they have to kick and cough up the football?"

Midland did not keep the drive going. Al Haney slammed into the line again but the defense held. The ball was a half-yard short of first down.

"Go for it! . . . Ram it down their throats! . . . Sock it to 'em! . . . Go!"

The man at the IST mike said, "The usual defiant yells from Midland fans. . . . Twenty-five, thirty, fifty thousand coaches, you name the figure," the telecaster said. "They don't have to live with a failure that might cost a ball game. They can yell for a team to go, yell for some favorite player to be put into the game, and—well, that's why coaches get gray hair, trying to satisfy rabid fans but still keep rational control of their team."

Mountain State stopped the Midland drive and forced a punt. They took over. The television man kept up a running comment.

"Mountain State operates almost strictly from the Pro Set, which means that they split one end, play another tight to his tackle (and this can vary from side to side) and station one back out as a flanker for receiving passes while the ground attack is given over to two running backs. They also use the man-in-motion, one back moving laterally behind the line—frequently the flanker—off a full-house backfield.

"There's the man-in-motion, but it's a quick-opening play through guard. Midland's defense was not fooled. Give the ball carrier a yard at most. They snap into formation again. The quarterback fades. It's a pass 'way down field! It is—incomplete! Mountain State is on the third-down hook now."

The Mountain State pass was again knocked down incomplete. They punted. Martin and Carnes and Haney made a first down, then Whitey took a short pass out in the flat for a twelve-yard gain and a second first down in a row on the Midland forty-eight.

". . . . Midland is rolling again, fans!" The telecaster cried into his microphone. "They come out of the huddle. Barr on the option, pitches out to Carnes. . . . Hank Ewing pulls from his guard spot to lead the interference and Hutch Kennedy is playing in as a tight end on that side . . . Carnes is running wide. . . . he is—"

"Cut, cut in, you dope! That end is too cagy to be turned . . ." Brad Barton talked to himself. The television man recapitulated the play. "The Mountain State end hand-fought blockers and drifted with the interference. The cornerback came up and knocked Carnes out of bounds exactly at midfield."

Midland needed a yard and a half on fourth down and again Ryan, refusing to gamble, called a punt.

That was the way things went through the first quarter. And the second fifteen minutes was a carbon copy of the initial period. During a short time-out interval before the half, the man at the IST microphone got conversational with the audience-yet-to-be of this taped gridiron action.

"This game looks to your announcer like it could be one of those scoreless affairs that rarely occur in this age of high-scoring games. Mike Ryan has developed a Midland team that is mighty, mighty tough defensively. They have held Mountain State to a single first down thus far, and we saw the Big Green mountaineers push over three touchdowns last week against Atlantic U. On the other hand, Mountain State's defense was riddled by Atlantic for six touchdowns—and Midland has not come close to scoring today.

"Ryan's team shows flashes of offensive power, but there seems to be a vital part missing. Something always bogs to ruin their drives. Your announcer would venture that the missing part may be Brad Barton."

The half-time gun banged with Midland trying futilely to hit with passes. The TV sportscaster turned the microphone over to his color man for the between-halves talk, leaned against the back wall of the booth and worked on a soft drink brought from the convenience booth that R. C. Fletcher provided in the pressbox for all Midland Stadium games. He eyed Brad Barton's jacket.

"You're a football man, huh?" he said. "Incapacitated?"

"Touchy ankle," Brad said.

"This is IST's first taping of a Midland game for later airing," the television man said. "I haven't seen Barton play, don't know anything much about him. What kind of guy is he, really?"

"What do you mean?"

"Oh, pressbox scuttlebutt being batted around. Is Barton a prima-donna gent? How about the effect on the rest of the squad? Is it a fact that he flouts Ryan? What's the campus reaction to the Ryan-Barton feud?"

Brad Barton eyed the IST telecaster. He figured that he knew what the game was, now. "Corn!" Brad spat. "Nuts!"

"So the setup is that bad, I take it." The telecaster nodded. "I don't blame you for not putting dirty linen on the line, although this is strictly off the record with me. Too bad. From what I hear, this Barton has plenty on the ball and could make Midland a very tough team to beat in the conference. But if he is riding Mike Ryan for a fall, he's picked the wrong gent. I know Ryan. He operates strictly on the square with his players, but Mike Ryan will run any squad he coaches."

"Maybe into the ground," Barton muttered.

Midland kicked off to start the second half and the pattern of the game resumed where it had left off. Mountain State could make no appreciable dent in the Midland defense and had to kick the ball away. Carnes, Haney, Martin and Barr reeled off yardage, kept the play in rival territory as they had done at Old Dominion. But also as had been the case at Old Dominion, they could not keep a drive going. Something always stalled their attack. They did not get inside the Mountain State twenty-yard line.

The scoreboard registered a scoreless deadlock when the clock light on the scoreboard jumped into the fifth-from-final circuit in the fourth quarter.

"Fans," the telecaster said into his microphone, "it looks more and more as though there is going to be no scoring here today. Midland has the ball on their own sixteen, after a prodigious seventy-yard boot off the foot of Mountain State's kicking specialist. Just under six minutes of playing time remains. Of course, anything can happen in six minutes of a football game, but on past performance, Midland will need more than—there they come. Single-wing set, Carnes deep. It's Carnes carrying. He starts wide, cuts back into the line and—oh, man! Did that Martin ever throw a block! The mike must have picked up the sound of that collision! A linebacker was simply obliterated! They did not knock Carnes off his feet until he was across the thirty!"

Midland reeled off two more first downs. They did it with a crunching ground attack off the tackles and inside the guards. The second first-down effort required the full four downs, but they were in Mountain State land.

"Hold everything, fans," the TV man chirped. "This Midland offense is clicking. Keep your fingers crossed, Midland supporters. . . . Ryan is sending in the plays. . . . Maybe Midland can forget that their ace is not in uniform. . . ."

Al Haney smashed for four yards. Barr faked to Haney, sneaked into a slit of daylight between guard and center for three. Martin hit off tackle for first down. It was tough, slam-bang football with Mountain State stubbornly fighting, yielding yardage grudgingly and slowly.

"They come out of the huddle, chattering, slapping each other on the backs. . . . that's a fired-up TEAM down there! The ball rests on the eight-yard line, the closest either team has been to pay dirt. Less than a minute remains. . . .

"It's Haney! . . . He rams off-tackle in a power

drive that looks like—like—yes, the referee puts the ball down on the four-yard line. Midland is inside the five—three downs to make four yards! . . . Haney slams at the same spot again. He made very little. . . . he made a yard. Third and three for a t.d. . . . . Midland hustles from the huddle; time is short. It's Haney again! It's awful close—awful close, fans. You'll know from the roar if it is a touchdown. . . . It isn't, it's not over. That Mountain State defense is rugged! Fourth down, last chance. What will it be? What would you call if you were the quarterback?

"There they come. Power-I set, Haney back. Midland is pinning their hopes on the man who carried the load. Barr has the snap from Turk Lauter, hands off to Haney driving toward the tackle spot and there is a big pileup. I don't think he made it. I don't think—hold everything! It IS a touchdown! A touchdown for Midland and we were fooled as much as. . . ."

The crowd roar drowned out the telecast for seconds as the referee ran over to the side opposite the squirming, battling pile of players and took the ball from Chuck Carnes. When the crowd noise subsided sufficiently, the I S T man spoke wonderingly into his mike.

"We'll try to explain while the teams line up for the conversion try. I would have taken oath that Barr stuck the ball into Haney's midriff. But he faked the handoff beautifully, hid the ball from the defense while he pivoted so he faced away from the line and slid the ball to Carnes. Carnes slipped along behind the line and stepped into the end zone without a hindering hand touching him when Whitey Martin banged the Mountain State cornerback definitely out of the picture.

"Carnes gets credit for the touchdown and Barr handled play selection masterfully in that drive. But, fans, we pay tribute to Whitey Martin. He sparked the drive. We have never seen Barton play, but if Martin is only Barton's back-up man—well, we venture the prediction that Barton will have to be super to oust Martin from the starting backfield!"

The game ended, the television man restated the Midland, 7; Mountain State, 0 final score and signed off. Then he turned to his spotters and thanked them. He said to Brad, "Looks to me as though Mike Ryan holds a big ace now. Ryan is that kind of guy. Men play over their heads for him because they recognize he's solid. I hope your Brad Barton sees the light."

Brad's eyes flashed black fire as he glared at the IST man.

"Break it off," Brad snapped. "You haven't fooled anybody with your corny performance. Tell Ryan for me that he wasted a built-up thing stuffing you full. I see the light, all right!"

He wheeled and slammed out of the television booth. The IST man stared slack-jawed at the door, then looked at the Mountain State spotter. "Was that really Brad Barton?" he asked.

"Yeah." The Mountain State youth shrugged. "I

played against him two years ago in a freshman game. I thought you knew, were—were—well, needling him for a little missionary work for Ryan."

"How about that?" The television man shook his head. Then he shrugged. "Well, maybe it will do Barton some good at that. But you were both wrong. Mike Ryan doesn't need anyone to front for him, chum. Barton can learn that the hard way!"

CHAPTER TWELVE

Will You Please Get Conscious?

It was Homecoming Week on the Midland campus.

Fraternity and sorority houses and dormitories were all decked out in blue and white banners and streamers. There were gay signs. *Welcome, Alumni. Welcome, Atlantic U.* A huge plasterboard tableau covered the front of East Dorm. It represented a football player in the blue and white of Midland running rampant with a football tucked under his arm, a sprawled figure in the crimson and silver of Atlantic U at the end of the ball carrier's straight arm. BEAT ATLANTIC'S CRIMSON WAVE was lettered above the Midland player in alternate letters of blue and white and below was FIGHT! TEAM! FIGHT!

It was Homecoming Week on Midland U campus.

Coach Mike Ryan customarily devoted Monday practice period following a game to viewing the game-film, pointing out missed assignments, mistakes and play deserving praise. Then every player who had seen game action and was healthy—no bad bruises or abrasions requiring ministrations of the trainer—ran one lap around the field, sprinted forty yards under the clocking of a coach, and was excused. Squad members not seeing game action received the attention of the coaching staff and the practice session concluded with a thirty-minute scrimmage.

Monday following the Mountain State game was different.

Chuck Carnes, Whitey Martin, Turk Lauter and Hutch Kennedy of the offensive unit, Dick Danner and Bert Long, free and strong safety of the defensive platoon, were absent when the squad straggled into the projection room. Neither was Coach Mike Ryan present when an assistant closed the door.

"Long's roommate is a basketball man," the assistant coach said. "Last Tuesday he went with Coach Ryan to a Boys' Club to demonstrate basket-shooting technique. He felt lousy yesterday and finally went to Student Health Center. He's over at University Hospital, now—with measles. Unfortunately. Carnes, Martin, Lauter, Kennedy and Danner were with Long and his roommate a considerable time Saturday night. They were all exposed to measles, so they are all being checked at the Health Center. Coach Ryan has been certified as immune, but he has gone to alert the Boys' Club officials."

The assistant coach shook his head and went on. "Not the best time for a half-dozen regulars to be exposed to measles, if there would be *any* best time. But most of them think maybe they've had measles when they were kids, or had immunization shots. Health Center people can't take chances on maybe, so until they check back home with their doctors and records, those six guys are barred from practice.

"That leaves things up in the air. It might be we have to juggle people around and maybe ask some of you to play both offense and defense in the Atlantic game. With that possibility in mind, we're going to try various normally offense-unit men at the safety spots for the defense."

Brad Barton worked longer at strong safety than any other player who was primarily offense. He knew from reactions of the coaches that he fitted in very well. Why not? he asked himself. I can play safety or cornerback or whatever—it's a matter of coordination and reaction.

The Student Health Center gave Lauter, Carnes, Danner, Martin and Kennedy okay-for-practice and they were suited out Tuesday. But Midland's defense platoon would be without the services of their strong safety. Long joined his roommate in the Isolation Ward at University Hospital.

Whitey Martin and Brad Barton divided practice

time between left halfback in the Wishbone-T and
Power-I offensive formations, and playing strong safety
in the defensive secondary.

Thursday Barton was at the defensive spot much
more than in the offensive backfield. At the close of the
workout he was convinced that Mike Ryan meant to
hand him another brush-off. Brad was in a very down
mood when he ran into R. C. Fletcher outside the
fieldhouse.

"Well, Brad!" Fletcher boomed. "I hope you're
all primed to give our alumni a good show Saturday."

In that moment Brad knew that the Graduate
Manager of Athletics had arranged this "running
into." He shrugged and said gloomily, "You can't put
on much of a show when you're on the bench half the
time!"

R. C. Fletcher gave him a sharp look, then spoke
in a grim tone. "I have not been unaware of Ryan's
unorthodox handling of certain matters," the Graduate Manager said. "A conference with Ryan is definitely indicated. Come along."

Mike Ryan looked sharply at Fletcher and his potential All American when they entered his office. He
did not appear surprised; but neither did he appear to
be at all on the defensive.

"There seems to be some doubt that you are going
to play Brad Saturday," Fletcher said without pream-
ble. "His ankle has fully recovered?"

Ryan nodded. "The trainer says it has."

"Well?"

"Well what? Barring unforeseen contingencies, I plan to play Barton."

"Where? When?"

"Wherever and whenever he will do the team the most good."

R. C. Fletcher eyed the coach a moment, then said, "The Atlantic game is a sellout. It is the first time we have ever sold out the entire stadium for a midseason game, even for Homecoming. You realize, of course, that thousands of alumni and Midland U followers ordered tickets expecting to see Brad Barton play."

"Possibly. I hadn't given that angle any particular thought."

"It's time you did, Ryan! A wise man does not hide his big attraction on the bench. Bluntly, Ryan, I must say that the whole matter of public relations has been handled very poorly on your part."

"Probably." A certain weariness was in Ryan's voice. "I never made claim to being a showman; I'm only a football coach." He eyed Brad Barton and added quietly, "I hadn't figured you for a cry-baby act."

Brad flushed. His black eyes snapped. But before he could say anything, R. C. Fletcher went on. "I demand your assurance that Barton will start against Atlantic and that he will be kept in the backfield the major portion of the game!"

Mike Ryan swivelled his eyes to the Graduate Manager. He did not say a word for seconds. When he did speak, his tone was soft but in no way groveling.

"You demand," he repeated. "Let me remind you again that I signed a contract to coach with no—but we have been over that thoroughly before. I give you this assurance: whatever men can do the most for Midland's team, in my judgment, will start the game. Martin has given us everything he has, gone out all the way every minute. His play in the Mountain State game certainly earned him consideration for a starting assignment against Atlantic. Martin and other kids are out there giving all they have for the team, all the time!" Mike Ryan eyed Brad Barton and the look in his eyes did not make Brad feel exactly comfortable. Ryan repeated, "All they have for the team, all the time."

R. C. Fletcher said stiffly, "You may regret this mulishness, Ryan!"

"It could be." Ryan lifted his shoulders in a shrug. "We seem to have said all that is necessary, I think."

Brad left the coach's office a trifle subdued, but the more he considered the encounter, the more angry he became. Ryan was more than mulish. He was—*not a rationalizer. Look who's calling who mulish!* Oh, shut up!

The Midland squad was due to pile into a bus at nine-thirty and head for quarters at the Country Club, miles away from the noise and revelry that would hold the campus. Ryan relaxed the rules to allow squad members to view the parade of Homecoming floats through the downtown streets and around the campus. The huge pile of wooden crates, boxes and anything else flammable that students had gathered behind the fieldhouse would be touched off at 8:45.

Brad Barton told himself that all this hoopla was a lot of corn. But no matter what he thought, the spirit of things seeped into him. He begged off when Whitey Martin invited him to accompany Turk Lauter, Al Haney and Steve Barr to watch the parade, then sneaked out alone to view the elaborate floats. He stood in the shadow around a corner of the fieldhouse when the bonfire was lighted, heard the yell for a speech from Coach Ryan. He listened to Ryan promise that the team would be out there tomorrow fighting in the Midland U tradition.

The team! The team! The team!

Oh, sure, you have to have a team to play football. But in the final analysis it always came down to individual effort. That was the rub. Mike Ryan refused to recognize that individuals made up his team. He did not want any player to stand out. He wanted only Mike Ryan to be the Big Cheese as developer of a team!

And you maybe ought to chew that over a couple of hundred times, too.

The inner voice repeated almost word for word the advice that Whitey Martin gave after the Tunsani game.

Shut up!

Anybody would have to be blind not to see that the offense clicked, was smoother and more effective with Brad Barton in there!

In the varsity dressing room beneath the stadium, Mike Ryan finished his final summing up of Atlantic's strengths and weaknesses as revealed in scouting reports.

"The coaching staff believes you can take them," he finished. "Our game plan is to control the ball, resort to passing only if they are caught in poor defense alignment or prove that we can't run against them. I think we can."

Then he said, "Atlantic won the toss; we're kicking to them. Martin will kick off, then come right out to rest a little before we go on offense."

He said not a word about the defense unit. Which means that Barton is pushed down the bench again, Brad thought bitterly. Whitey Martin followed Brad from the dressing room and jogged even with him in the tunnel to the playing field.

"This one really counts," Whitey said. "This is one we really want to put it all together for!"

"Yeah!" The word came out almost a snarl. "Put it all together—hah! All together for Ryan, Martin and the DAILY COLLEGIAN!"

The instant the words were out, Brad was appalled. Why had he said a thing like that? Whitey Martin looked up quickly, held his gaze a moment, then shook his head.

"If I didn't pity you so much, that crack would burn me plenty," Whitey said. "For gosh sakes, will you please get conscious?"

CHAPTER THIRTEEN

Homecoming

WHITEY MARTIN usually powered the ball into the rival end zone when he kicked off. But this time he did not come anywhere near the end zone. Whether he missed the rhythm of his approach run, or whether it was just one of those things that occasionally happen to the best of kickers, there was no doubt that Whitey foozled that kick.

The ball squirted off the side of his foot about six feet high and sliced toward the sideline. It hit a shoulder pad of one of the Atlantic linemen stationed ahead of their forty-five yard line and before the surprised forward could clutch it, the leather oval slanted back toward the center of the field.

Once a kickoff has traveled ten yards the ball may be fielded by any player of either team and advanced —one of the few times rules allow a member of the kicking team to run with a recovered kick. Whitey Martin grabbed the oval. He raced straight ahead through the momentarily confused Atlantic forward line then cut sharply right.

Blockers mowed down three Atlantic men speeding to close the open lane and a great deceptive move left another lunging effort short. Big Turk Lauter rumbled behind Whitey as one of the Atlantic backs who had been deep to receive the kickoff angled across to pinch Whitey out of bounds.

"Cut in and slow a little," Lauter gasped, "so I have a shot at him!"

Lauter's devastating block catapulted the Atlantic back a yard outside the playing field. Whitey Martin rode the exultant roar from alumni, students and plain fans into the end zone and Midland had a touchdown in the first fifteen seconds. Whitey Martin booted the conversion try squarely between the uprights; Midland, 7; Atlantic, 0.

A bad break like that can ruin a team, but it did not faze Atlantic. They received again, took Martin's kick two yards deep in the end zone and ran the ball out to their thirty-two.

They cut loose a pair of hard-driving backs, mixed line smashes, off-tackle slants and sweeps, all run from their pro-set type offense. They made three first downs in succession. Then their quarterback saw the Midland strong safety playing in too far, backing up the line. He fired a sharp pass to his tight end breaking into the poorly covered area, hit him and the play was good for a twenty-six yard gain. First down at the Midland six.

Midland dug in. They stopped two slashes at the tackles for negligible gain. They threw back a trap up the middle short of the payoff line by no more than ten inches.

"Hold that line! Hold that line! Hold that line!"

Midland supporters pleaded. Linebackers, cornerbacks and safeties bunched into what amounted to an eleven-man front designed to pile up the fourth-down play.

They did not pile it up.

Atlantic's quarterback faked a handoff to his fullback barrelling into the line, spun and tossed a pass to his flankerback. The flanker stepped over the goal line for the touchdown. They converted the point after touchdown try and it was a new ball game, 7–7.

That was all the scoring in the first half until twenty seconds before the half-time gun. Atlantic clearly had the offensive edge, and rang up four more first downs while Midland seemed powerless to put together any consistent attack. More than a few times there were spots when a well-placed pass, or a sparkling run might have touched off Midland. Each time Brad Barton looked hopefully toward Coach Mike Ryan. Brad was primed to go, straining at the well-known leash. But Mike Ryan gave him not a notice.

Carnes was sent in to relieve Whitey Martin and Whitey shifted to the defense unit to play strong safety. Martin played inspired ball. But for him, Atlantic would have surely counted at least another touchdown. But even a tough, rugged man can tire in a setup like that. Whitey Martin slowed noticeably in the waning minutes of the second quarter.

Atlantic took over possession of the ball on their own thirty and in six plays were on the Midland twenty-nine, first down. They threw the same pass that scored their touchdown. Whitey Martin somehow got over in time to bat the pass incomplete. Then Atlantic came right back with a carbon copy of the same aerial pattern and this time Martin just did not get there in time. First down on the nine.

Midland called time out. On the bench Brad Barton was sure that Ryan would send him in to replace Whitey. He had to, Whitey was almost completely bushed.

Coach Ryan sent in the man who had started at strong safety.

Atlantic hammered at the touchdown door, ripped and smashed to the two-yard line in three plays. Two seconds of playing time left to the half showed on the clock, time for one play.

Hold 'em, gang! Brad Barton was surprised to find himself mouthing the words. A slender player ran out from the Atlantic bench, their kicking specialist.

He stood back on the ten-yard line and calmly lifted a perfect field goal over the desperately leaping Midland linemen. Scoreboard figures changed to Atlantic, 10; Midland, 7 as the first half ended.

Brad confidently expected Ryan to send him into the game to start the second half. No matter whether offense or defense, Big Cheese had to see that he was needed out there. But Ryan announced that the same men would start the third period that had been in at the end of the half.

Midland received, managed to get a first down, lost yardage on two plays and went into kick formation. Atlantic brought Whitey Martin's punt to their thirty-nine and started again. They were in the midst of a drive when a fumble stopped them at the Midland forty.

But the Midland attack still was not hitting and Martin punted again. Atlantic took possession on their twelve. They began to grind steadily upfield. Ryan sent in a replacement for Martin at safety. Atlantic completed a pass in the strong safety's zone on the first play.

"Martin!" Coach Ryan called down the bench. "Get back in there. You've got to watch that pass to their tight end!"

Brad Barton ran the gamut of emotions, but above all a driving, demanding desire for action built in him. It came to him suddenly that not once during this game had the student cheering section yelled, "We want Barton!" Had Randy Fletcher's campaign convinced the student body that Barton was a stinker?

Couldn't Ryan see that Martin was practically through? Playing both offense and defense was killing him. The team was in danger of falling apart. A fresh, capable man in there could make all the difference.

Well, do you know a capable man big enough to—

Shut up! Brad never was sure whether he shouted silently or aloud to the plaguing inner voice. Strange emotions roiled inside him. Abruptly he shucked off his warm-up jacket. Then he crouched in front of Coach Ryan.

"You've got to put me in! You've got to!"

Ryan stabbed a look at him, said nothing, pushed Barton aside so he could see out on the field. A ball carrier roared through a gaping hole and into the Midland secondary. Whitey Martin made the tackle. The ball was just inside the five-yard line. Whitey Martin arose slowly, staggered as he walked toward his position.

"Put me in," Brad pleaded. "Whitey's out on his feet!"

"Do you want in there for Brad Barton or for Midland?"

"The team needs me!"

Something flickered in Ryan's eyes. "You're in," he said softly. "Report for Martin."

Whitey Martin peered glassily at his former

roommate. "I'm gambling on Barton," he muttered thickly. "He'll be in the game the minute he shows me he wants to play for Midland first and Barton second. I still believe he's solid underneath and will come through, but you'll be carrying the load until he does."

Brad stared at Martin. Migosh, the beating he'd taken had made him goofy! Whitey grinned painfully.

"What Coach told me before the game," he said. "Welcome back. Go get 'em, Brad!"

"Let's go, everybody!" Barton cried. "Hang tough! Rock 'em and sock 'em!"

Weary linemen settled cleats into the turf. Brad watched the Atlantic quarterback closely. At the snap of the ball, Brad shot over the line. He hit the ball carrier a second's fraction after the quarterback made the handoff and it was very close to being fumbled. The Atlantic back barely managed to clutch the ball as he crumpled under Barton's driving bulk.

The referee placed the ball, said, "Third and goal to go." The leather oval rested five yards and a half from the double chalkmark now. Atlantic had lost more than a yard.

"Stick it to 'em!" Brad Barton yelled as he slapped linemen on their posteriors. "Take that thing away from 'em!"

He retreated a little. The quarterback would not expect another safety blitz. Brad shot forward again, timing his drive and hit the man he figured was the ball carrier. He had figured wrong. That quarterback was cool, poised and cagy. He simply side-stepped, drew the ball away from Barton's grasp and followed a blocker into a slit inside tackle. He lanced through for the touchdown on the side where Brad Barton should have been protecting.

They kicked the point and scoreboard figures jumped to Atlantic, 17; Midland, 7.

Brad Barton kicked disgustedly at the turf as the teams went upfield for the kickoff. "Hotshot, that's me," he berated himself. "I cost us that touchdown. Shaft the barbs, you guys. I've got 'em coming!"

Players looked at him, looked at each other. Nobody could miss the bitter frustration in his eyes. "Forget it," somebody mumbled.

"Forget it is right." Whitey Martin had come out from the bench. "You were in there pitching. That t.d. won't whip us! Anybody think it will?"

Nobody voiced an opinion. They had been taking a terrific pounding for forty minutes. Pepper talk was all right, but. . . .

Brad Barton stood on the goal line. Never before had he wanted so intensely to tear off a long run, but he got no chance. Atlantic coaches had been warned by their scouts. They ordered their kicker to boot the ball away from Barton. It went to Al Haney and the fullback bulled straight up the middle to the fifteen-yard line.

In the huddle, Steve Barr said, "Coach didn't send a play!"

"Give me that apple," Brad Barton said. "I'm fresher than Haney or Martin."

Barr nodded. "Okay," he agreed. "It's 42A."

The off-tackle smash was the backbone of Mike Ryan's attack but it had been going nowhere this day. Atlantic had Midland well scouted and had consistently smothered Carnes and Martin. They almost smothered Brad Barton now.

The hole closed as he ripped into daylight; hands slapped at his thighs. But Brad Barton had that something extra that other Midland backs lacked this day. He spun from the arms of a linebacker, stiff-armed another tackle try by the cornerback and used him as a fulcrum to pivot clear. He sliced through the Atlantic secondary and when he was finally knocked out of bounds his cleats dug whiting from the twenty-five yard line.

"Give me that thing again," he said in the huddle. "Keep giving it to me!"

He hit the opposite tackle and drove through for six yards. He got three more on a cutback when the hole off tackle was blocked. Steve Barr gave Haney the ball to allow Brad a breather and the fullback bulled to a first down with a yard to spare. The Midland stands came suddenly alive.

"Go, Midland, go! . . . Roll, Blue and White, roll! . . . Yea, team, GO!"

Back to Brad. He started on 42B as though he was going to hit off-tackle, then as a linebacker closed the gate, Brad veered out. His change of pace fooled the wide defensive man and he turned the corner. He barreled down the sideline across midfield, broke a tackle thrown by the last Atlantic man who was a threat to stop him, but stepped out of bounds in eluding the tackle try.

"Fight, fight! Blue and White! . . . Fight, fight! Blue and White! . . . Go, team, go! . . . Yea-a-a, team!"

Now the going began to get really tough. Atlantic was aroused to the fact that Midland's attack had suddenly become potent. They stopped Haney for a scant yard gain; they slowed Barton in two slashes off tackle and it was fourth down and four to go.

"They'll expect a pass," Brad said in the huddle. "If Coach hasn't sent in a play, cross 'em, Steve. How about faking me on 28 and Whitey carries?"

"Coach hasn't sent in a play since you came in." Steve Barr's tone held a kind of puzzlement. He frowned. "It's dangerous trying to outsmart them here, though."

Barr looked at his team. Eyes were alight; weary shoulders were straightened. Abruptly the quarterback said, "In the bag! That's it, gang. 28."

They had not tried 28 throughout the game. It was a simple naked reverse, depending for success on the unexpectedness of a back carrying the ball against the flow of the play with not a single blocker in front of him. It unwound as Mike Ryan might have drawn it on a blackboard before installing the reverse.

Brad took Barr's pitchout, swerved back two steps,

arm cocked as though he was going to pass, then he
darted right as though carrying on a sweep. Ray Parson pulled from his guard position and headed wide as
though leading interference for the ball carrier. Brad
slipped the ball to Whitey Martin as they criss-crossed
and the ball-handling was as neat as he had ever per-
formed when he played quarterback. The Atlantic defense was completely taken in by the fake. Even as they
swarmed Brad Barton down, Whitey Martin legged it
around the opposite side. Whitey reached the fifteen-
yard line before a safety man forced him out of bounds.

Barton slashed off-tackle for four yards. Back
again inside the same spot for three. Tough, tough
yards now. Haney barged into the center of the line,
short of a first down. The third period ended and
Whitey Martin walked beside Brad Barton as the
teams changed ends of the field.

"You're more than a shot in the arm," Whitey
said. "You can win for us again."

"Sure we'll win it—all of us!"

They did not win it right then, but they climbed
decidedly back into the ball game on the first play of
the fourth quarter. Brad crouched in the left halfback
spot in the Wishbone-T. Steve Barr had called for a
halfback pass and suddenly Brad was mentally seeing
Mike Ryan standing behind the reserve line and calling the shots on what Brad Barton was going to do.
Brad did not know whether he might be tightening the
fingers of his passing hand and did not dare look, but

he willed himself to relax all over. No tipoff today. And somebody in the defensive backfield was keeping tabs. As Barr pivoted to make the pitch back to Brad, some defensive man yelled, "No pass! He's going to run it!"

That false warning helped make the play a cinch. Brad ran five steps hard, faking a sweep, swerved suddenly and rifled a pass to Whitey Martin cutting across behind the defensive back. Whitey went all the way and the stands exploded with wild yells. They kept on exploding while Barr held and Whitey booted the extra point.

Now it was only 17–14 for Atlantic.

Atlantic players were grim as they spread out for the kickoff. They were fully aroused, for they knew they were no longer dominating Midland. They brought the ball back to their twenty-eight after the kick. They opened their bag of plays and turned loose the power of a diversified attack.

Off tackle for four yards; a spinning back crashed over guard for three; first down on a cutback from a sweep. A short pass over the line, complete. A long pass batted down. They shook a ball carrier loose on a quick-opener from a T-set and he rambled to the Midland thirty-five. Brad Barton again found himself in front of Mike Ryan.

"Coach," he pleaded, "send me in. I can go both ways the rest of the game." He grinned crookedly and added, "A guy can store up a big reserve of energy riding the bench!"

He was not sure but he thought he caught the ghost of an amused glint in Ryan's eyes. The coach said, "Get out there!"

Brad Barton was a ball of fire, making slamming tackles, slapping teammates on the back, hurling fight talk. The team was weary but something was happening that had not been apparent before. The fire of Barton's play, his fight was welding them into a more spirited unit. They forced Atlantic to try for a fourth-down pass and Brad read the play all the way. He took no chance of maybe being out-fought for possession if he tried to intercept. He batted the ball across the end zone sideline.

Midland's ball on the twenty-yard stripe. Then came a bad break. Barr mistimed a handoff to Haney and Atlantic recovered the fumble at the nineteen. They snapped confidently from the huddle.

Slam, batter, bam! Bone-shaking blocks, tooth-rattling tackles. The teams battled down there at the bottom of a roaring stadium.

Atlantic did not score. Midland took the ball on downs at the nine when Atlantic elected to go for first down with only inches to make, instead of trying a field goal. Then began the heart-stopping task of slogging ninety-one yards to the touchdown Midland had to have for a win.

Time ground away. The scoreboard clock showed five minutes left to play, then four, then three, then two minutes—and the ball was only at the Atlantic forty-eight. Atlantic went into their prevent defense, playing loose, willing to allow short yardage gains but covering against a long bomb—a scoring pass—or having a ball carrier break for a long gainer. Time was definitely working now for Atlantic.

Brad wondered afterward why he was suddenly again thinking of Mike Ryan calling plays he was going to make before he made them. He was working hard to eliminate the faults that tipped the rival defense, but he remembered that in the heat of the Tunsani game he had lapsed into the old habit. It could happen again; those Atlantic guys had shown they keyed on him, watched for tipoffs. That was when the big idea came. He clutched Turk Lauter's arm.

"Call a time-out," Brad said. The captain looked at him questioningly. "I've got a brainstorm that'll score for us the easy way. Tell Barr to trot over and ask the—ask Coach Ryan if we can pull something different."

Steve Barr said, "Coach told me when we were on the bench that he wasn't going to send plays the rest of the way."

Captain Turk Lauter called time. Midland players gathered around him and Brad.

"We'll sucker them," Brad said. "Good." He outlined his plan.

"Sounds okay," Lauter said. "Do we go along with it, gang?"

"With one change," Whitey Martin said.

Brad turned on him, "Why change? It's a cinch to score for us again and—"

"But you'll do the scoring," Whitey said. He looked around at his teammates. "How about it? Has he earned it?"

"Check! . . . You said it! . . . Yeah." Not a disagreeing sound.

"I've scored two touchdowns this game—TWO! Great day!" Whitey cracked a grin through the sweat-mud grime that masked his face. "Here's what we do: instead of you standing back there and deliberately tipping that you're going to run, then pitching me a pass, you give the tip that it's going to be a pass, only it won't be. They'll be remembering the other time and just a little unsure, so things ought to be better. You run it all the way. Get him past the front guys, gang, and Al and I'll mop up the secondary!"

"Right! . . . It's in the bag! . . . The old pepper! . . . We've got 'em!"

Brad Barton felt wonderful as he crouched in his stance. These guys were a great gang. Mike Ryan had forged them into a—he stopped short. What do you know, *me* thinking of Mike Ryan without resentment! How about that?

He hoped the coach was watching and saw him tighten the fingers of his throwing hand until the knuckles whitened. Ryan would be fit to be tied. He hoped the defense was watching him, too.

Turk Lauter handed the ball back to Barr and as the quarterback turned and pitched back to Brad, a linebacker yelled, "Pass! Pass! Watch the halfback pass!"

The secondary spread, tacked onto Hutch Kennedy, Mick Rooney and Whitey Martin. The backer-upper in the middle glued himself to Al Haney as the fullback barged through the line.

Things could not have worked out better. Brad put on a convincing show of looking frantically for a receiver until the hard-charging front-four of the defense were fully committed. Then suddenly he was side-stepping, dodging, and his speed left the linemen chasing him forlornly. He rounded the flank as somebody put a tie-up block on the Atlantic cornerback and barreled into a broken field.

It was not a broken field very long—it was a completely clear field. Kennedy, Rooney, Haney and Martin—covered as potential pass receivers—suddenly reversed the tables and became blockers. There was not an Atlantic man on his feet within twenty yards of Brad Barton as his legs pistoned over the chalkmarks. He circled into the end zone, dropped the ball on the ground and grinned at an Atlantic man who had been chasing him dejectedly.

That was the ball game. The scoreboard registered a 21–17 margin for Midland when the final gun sounded a few plays later with Atlantic trying desperately to connect on long passes, and having them batted down by a defense suddenly as alert as though the game was just beginning.

Players ran for the dressing-room tunnel. Fans

poured from the stands. Randy Fletcher had come down from the pressbox and stood at the tunnel mouth. Brad Barton loved everybody in the world, and he had a sneaking conviction that Randy had given the initial push to the wave of things that finally rolled some sense into Brad Barton.

Brad rumpled the DAILY COLLEGIAN editor's hair, said, "How about running something about that one in your campus scandal sheet!"

"Wait till you see Monday's DAILY! You really were something else out there!"

"Something else different." Brad sobered momentarily. "Thanks, Randy!"

Then there were scores of youngsters, shoving programs at Brad, begging for his autograph. He scribbled his name, grinning, loving all of it. He was suddenly aware that Mike Ryan stood a few yards away, watching. R. C. Fletcher was behind Ryan. The Graduate Manager had lost his hat but looked as though he could not have cared less. Ryan's battered hat was firmly on his head but set somehow different. Midland wins and Mr. Fletcher is happy, Brad thought. They'll get along, Mr. Fletcher needs somebody to face up to him like I need a coach that won't stand for anybody coaching the coach.

"Come on over, Coach," Brad cried, "and bring Mr. Fletcher. These people ought to have your autographs!"

He looked squarely at Ryan then and his black

eyes sparkled. "Maybe the whole squad ought to get daubed with a little glamour—Coach!"

Whitey Martin got the subtle surrender and he saw that Coach Mike Ryan did not miss it. Whitey said in a tone of mock dismay, "Once a glamour-boy, always a glamour-boy! Man, teams on the rest of our schedule are in real trouble, now! What a homecoming!"

Ryan's gray eyes held Barton's black ones and there was nothing ghostly about the smile that wrinkled the coach's features. He said, "A real homecoming, for all of us."